MURDER IN HYDE PARK

A GINGER GOLD MYSTERY # 14

LEE STRAUSS

Copyright © 2020 by Lee Strauss

Cover by Steven Novak

Illustrations by Tasia Strauss

All rights reserved.

No part of this book may be reproduced in any form or by any electronic or mechanical means, including information storage and retrieval systems, without written permission from the author, except for the use of brief quotations in a book review.

Library and Archives Canada Cataloguing in Publication

Title: Murder in Hyde Park / Lee Strauss.

Names: Strauss, Lee (Novelist), author.

Series: Strauss, Lee (Novelist). Ginger Gold mystery ; 14.

Description: Series statement: A Ginger Gold mystery ; 14 | "A 1920s cozy historical mystery."

Identifiers: Canadiana (print) 20200283731 | Canadiana (ebook) 2020028374X | ISBN 9781774091319

(hardcover) | ISBN 9781774091296 (softcover) | ISBN 9781774091302 (IngramSpark softcover) | ISBN

9781774091272 (Kindle) | ISBN 9781774091289 (EPUB)

Classification: LCC PS8637.T739 M85 2020 | DDC C813/.6—dc23

❦ Created with Vellum

GINGER GOLD MYSTERIES
(IN ORDER)

Murder on the SS *Rosa*
Murder at Hartigan House
Murder at Bray Manor
Murder at Feathers & Flair
Murder at the Mortuary
Murder at Kensington Gardens
Murder at St. George's Church
The Wedding of Ginger & Basil
Murder Aboard the Flying Scotsman
Murder at the Boat Club
Murder on Eaton Square
Murder by Plum Pudding
Murder on Fleet Street
Murder at Brighton Beach

Murder in Hyde Park
Murder at the Royal Albert Hall
Murder in Belgravia

1

The grand Summer Fashion Show, set in Hyde Park, was only one day away, and Feathers & Flair was abuzz with energy. In the back room of the Regent Street dress shop belonging to Mrs. Ginger Reed, last-minute details were being attended to. A red-velvet curtain hid the mayhem from the sophistication of the display room on the other side. Madame Roux, the shop manager, fussed and clicked her tongue, giving clipped French-accented instructions to Millie, the long and lithe model, to dress quickly and see to the customer standing by the tall windows awaiting a demonstration.

"A fashion show may be in our future, Miss

Tatum," Madame Roux said, "but we have customers today!"

Millie, dressed in a new, sparkling silk gown the colour of sea glass and as wispy as seaweed, passed through the velvet curtain to the vast display room with its shiny white-marble floors, high ceilings trimmed in gold, and lit with an electric chandelier. Dorothy West, the young shop attendant who lacked the model's level of sophistication, assisted.

Ginger turned to her resident seamstress and designer, Emma Miller. A former student of fashion design, Miss Miller showed tremendous potential, and it was Ginger's secret concern the girl would get a better offer and leave Feathers & Flair.

"They're a whirlwind of excitement, aren't they, Emma?" Ginger said.

For what seemed like the thousandth time, Emma scrutinised the rack of frocks—her own designs—ready for the fashion runway.

"Oh, madam, I don't blame them. I'm quite flushed myself. Whenever I think of the show, and all the famous designers coming . . ." She ran a slender hand across her brow. "Especially Coco Chanel! Will she be there? Have you heard?"

Ginger bit her cheek to keep from grinning.

Emma's nerves shone through her uncharacteristic chattering.

"Mademoiselle Chanel isn't one to make commitments, I'm afraid," Ginger said. "Although, I've heard from the event organisers that her mannequins and designs are on their way, if one can believe the French."

Ginger often envied the *joie de vivre* of her French counterparts, their flair for life, and their little regard for rules or propriety. Being English could be rather dull in comparison.

Emma gasped. "Do you think we'll see the little black dress?"

Coco Chanel had debuted the controversial frock that spring to the dismay of many and the delight of a few. Ginger counted herself among the latter.

"I certainly hope so," Ginger replied. Her hand caressed her growing belly. The colour black created the illusion of slimness, though at the rate her little one inside was growing, she could hardly imagine that any colour could mask her condition in due time. She was thankful that the current trends were for straight lines that dropped from the shoulder. The earlier cinch-waisted gowns of the previous generation would be far less forgiving.

"I adore her, Mrs. Reed," Emma said, her eyes glazed over as she placed her palms over her heart. "I shall simply die if she comes."

This time, Ginger couldn't hold back her laughter. "Well, that shall never do, Emma. We need you alive and well for this event. We have a lot of work to do."

Ginger braced herself to face the small mountain of correspondence waiting for her on her desk in the back room's tiny office. She held in a growing sense of frustration toward her former sister-in-law, Felicia Gold, who Ginger employed to help her in her investigative office around the corner. For this week, however, Ginger had asked for help in the dress shop, and Felicia had reassured her that she'd join in on the effort. But since she'd started stepping out with Lord Davenport-Witt, Felicia's word had begun to mean nothing. Ginger understood the draw of new love, but that didn't excuse one from keeping to one's word and responsibilities.

Wanting to finish her desk work before the afternoon postal delivery and pickup, Ginger picked up her fountain pen and wrote several responses to letters waiting. By the time she'd finished her task, her hand was cramped.

Madame Roux stepped into the office, looking flushed.

"How is everything on the floor?" Ginger asked. "Is everything all right?"

"*Oui, oui*. It's busy, and sales are brisk, but a new customer, one I've never seen before, has asked for you." Madame Roux's ski-jump nose pointed upwards. "She refused service from me. 'Only the owner,' she said."

How odd, Ginger thought. She got to her feet, a little less gracefully than had come naturally before she was with child, and smoothed out her skirt. She wore a pretty powder-blue day frock with a floral pattern and pearl detailing, and when she walked through the velvet curtains to meet their demanding customer, she was glad she looked her best.

Before her stood a petite but formidable-looking lady in a summer hat with a narrow brim, wide ribbon, and an abundance of felt roses. A fringe of grey hair peeked out along her lined forehead. Despite her years, her posture was so straight that only a corset could be responsible. The lines on her face were plentiful and deep; however, it was clear by her high cheekbones and facial structure that she had been a beauty in her youth. And, unlike many women in their later years, this lady had a good grasp of fashion and was wearing a soft-grey silk frock with flaring, pleated sleeves and a pleated, low-dropping skirt, tastefully highlighted with rose-coloured trim. Ginger recognised it as an Alice Bernard design she'd seen in a recent *La Femme Chic* magazine.

"Good afternoon," Ginger said, a friendly smile pasted on her face. She'd learned to keep her voice low to keep it from carrying along the high ceilings. "I'm Mrs. Reed, the owner of this establishment."

Ginger held out a hand, gloveless, but with fingers expertly manicured and a row of tasteful rings on her fingers.

The lady hesitated before accepting the handshake. "I'm Deborah, Duchess of Worthington. I was under the impression that a titled lady ran this shop."

The skin around Ginger's green eyes tightened. It was true. When she'd opened Feathers & Flair, her official legal title was Lady Gold, as widow of Lord Daniel Gold, a baron. Then she fell in love with Basil Reed. Though the grandson of a viscount, Basil worked as a chief inspector at Scotland Yard, which meant, to some, a slip down the ladder. However, Ginger had readily forfeited the title and the prestige that came with it to spend the rest of her life with him.

Most of the time, Ginger didn't miss it.

"Yes," Ginger answered politely. "But now it is run by me. Is there something I can help you find? We can order any of the latest fashions from all the esteemed designers, or our resident designer could help you with an original."

Ginger didn't bother to tell the highbrow lady that the upper floor contained racks of factory-made frocks, a new trend followed by the younger generation and those who appreciated the convenience of buying an outfit already sized, and that could be worn that very day.

"Are you new to London?" Ginger enquired. She'd encountered every lady of consequence in the city at some point.

"Until recently, my husband, the Duke of Worthington, and I lived in our villa in Morocco, but with the conflict there . . ." She flicked a hand as if she were bored with the subject. The Rif War between Spain's colonial power and the regional Berber tribes had been ongoing for six years. Tiring of it, all of Europe hoped for an end to the conflict soon. "The Duke is busy in Barcelona, so I came here."

She sniffed with an expression of displeasure. "London is still a rather filthy city, isn't it?"

Propriety insisted that Ginger take the insult to

her city on the chin. "There are many lovely places in London, and you might be interested in the fashion show coming to Hyde Park this Friday afternoon. It'll be splendid."

"Yes, I've heard about the event." She glanced around the shop and then back at Ginger. "Perhaps."

"Can I help you with your fashion needs, Your Grace?" Ginger asked, hoping to move this unpleasant encounter along.

"I think not. My driver is waiting in the motorcar. Coco Chanel's London shop is dazzling, and near my home in Mayfair, where I'm currently staying. Good day, Mrs. Reed."

Of course, Ginger knew of Coco Chanel's connections in the area, particularly her alleged affair with Bendor, 2nd Duke of Westminster.

The Duchess of Worthington turned on her heel, never laying an eye on Madame Roux who'd remained several steps behind Ginger, nor the shop girls that watched, wide-eyed, at the back.

"Well," Ginger said, facing her staff. "I doubt we'll see her again." To herself, she thought, *good riddance.*

The bell above the door rang as the postman entered.

"Dorothy," Ginger said, "be a brick and grab the outgoing letters on my desk."

"Good afternoon, Mrs. Reed," the postman said, handing her a bundle of letters. He waited until Dorothy returned, handing him the outgoing post. "Very good," he said. "Good day, ladies."

"He's a nice man, isn't he?" Dorothy said with a soft sigh.

"Too short for me," Millie quipped.

Ginger perused the post, stopping on one letter with a Paris return address. She recognised the neat cursive script. "Oh, Emma. I think it's her."

Emma stepped forward, her hands clasped highly in front of her frock. "*Her*, madam?"

Ginger removed the single card inserted inside and read aloud.

"My dearest Ginger." Ginger paused on the next word, the pet surname written behind her name, *LaFleur*. Withholding that, she continued. "I'm pleased to tell you that I shall be returning to London shortly and shall attend your little fashion show along with my entourage. I look forward to sharing a glass of chardonnay with you. And a grotesque basket of your famous fish and chips!"

"You didn't say that you and Mademoiselle

Chanel were friends," Madame Roux said. "Though I'm not surprised."

"We met in Paris, long ago—before her Chanel N°5 perfume shot her to fame and fortune." Ginger's mind went back to the moment they had met, before Ginger's recruitment into the British secret service, during what seemed another lifetime. Ginger would hardly call them friends.

Emma gripped the edge of the sales counter. "Coco Chanel is coming. I think I'm going to faint."

2

By the time Ginger made it back to Hartigan House for afternoon tea, she was knackered. She blamed her delicate condition, and her friend Matilda Hill, a former medical student, had previously confirmed Ginger's self-diagnosis. A little lie-down before tea had become a routine, and with the fashion show tomorrow, Ginger needed to conserve her energy.

Tapping the brake of her pearly-white Crossley, Ginger slowed as she rumbled down the lane behind her house, dust kicking up behind the vehicle. She skidded into the back garden, missing the lamp post, and pulled into the open garage door without denting the brass horn.

Clement, the gardener and sometimes chauffeur, dropped the clippers he was trimming the hedges with and hurried over to offer his assistance.

"No shopping bags today, madam?" he asked, barely concealing his surprise.

Ginger smiled. "I'm afraid I've come home empty-handed."

Instead of heading directly indoors, Ginger turned towards the small stable beyond the garage. Since receiving the happy news about her coming child, Ginger had been missing riding her beautiful gelding, Goldmine. Of the rare Akhal-Teke breed, the horse had golden hair, a flowing mane, and a cascading tail, reminiscent of a fairy tale. A warm breeze brought the scent of hay and horses from the direction of the small wood and stone stable, and Ginger headed over to say hello to the two horses that sheltered there.

"Is Scout in the stables?" Ginger asked Clement.

"No, madam. He and Mr. Reed have gone to play tennis."

"Oh, that's right." Ginger silently chastised her failing memory, another skill stilted by her condition. Matilda assured her that all things affecting her mind and body would right themselves once the baby was born. A young mother herself, Matilda's words comforted Ginger.

Ginger approached the stables, her ears perking up at the sound of low voices, soft and bubbly, cooing and giggling, coming from the building. Male and female.

Bracing herself, Ginger entered with a smile.

"Hello, Felicia," she said, having recognised her sister-in-law's laughter. The much younger sister of Ginger's late husband, Daniel, Felicia had a pretty tear-drop-shaped face; glossy brown hair styled in neat marcel waves; and mischievous looking eyes common to the flapper girls of the times.

Ginger acknowledged Felicia's companion with a polite nod. "Charles."

The Earl of Witt, known as Lord Davenport-Witt, turned on his charm. Tall with dark, brooding eyes and a smile that pulled up crookedly, he said, "Ginger! How are you this fine day?"

"Quite well, thank you."

Both Felicia and Charles were dressed in jodhpurs and blazers and held bridles in their hands.

"Charles and I are going to ride along the Serpentine. You don't mind, do you?"

Ginger felt her mouth twitch. She was quite possessive of Goldmine, but it was rather unfair to forbid others to ride him, especially when she could not. After all, he also needed exercise. She stroked the gelding's golden nose.

"Of course not." To Charles, she added, "I'm certain Basil won't mind if you ride Sir Blackwell."

Charles was already fitting the bridle on the auburn Arabian. "I'll bring him back in good shape, I assure you."

Setting her gaze on Felicia, Ginger sniffed. "I was expecting you in the shop today."

Felicia's fingers flew to her mouth. "I completely forgot! Charles rang, and . . ." She giggled. "It just left my mind. Do forgive me."

"Of course," Ginger said. "But you won't fail me tomorrow. I'm counting on you to help with the show."

"I'll be there," Felicia promised. "With bells on."

"I'll do my part to ensure Felicia doesn't forget," Charles said. His eyes lingered on Felicia with fondness.

"Very well," Ginger said. "I hope you have a good ride."

Ginger strolled along the stone walkway to the back entrance of Hartigan House. She felt unsettled. Ever since she'd met Charles Davenport-Witt whilst on holiday in Brighton, she'd not trusted him, though she couldn't conceive of why. He was charming, handsome, seemed to care for Felicia sincerely, and was an earl—something that made her former grandmother-in-law, Ambrosia, the Dowager Lady Gold, very happy.

For weeks, Ginger had wrestled with the foggy niggle in the back of her mind. Again, she blamed the delicacy of her condition for failing her. Frustrating as it was, she couldn't remember what it was about the earl that bothered her.

Then, on a stormy summer evening—thunder rolling and lightning flashing—it came to her. The earl hadn't lied, but he hadn't told her the full truth. Yes, he'd known Daniel, and yes, he'd served in the Great War in France in His Majesty's service.

But that wasn't all.

Ginger knew but wasn't telling. Not yet, and maybe never. And no doubt, Felicia would go through her life unaware, but there was nothing Ginger could do about that. Besides, it was possible the relationship between Felicia and Charles might come to nothing.

One could hope.

In full summer bloom, the flower garden surrounded the patio. Ambrosia sat in one of the chairs, pointing her silver-handled walking stick as she instructed her maid, Langley, to pick flowers.

"A mix of roses and irises. No, not that one, the one behind that. And take one of those white lilies."

Ginger couldn't help but feel a little sorry for Langley, whose brow shimmered with sweat. Had she seen the maid smile once since she came to live at Hartigan House with Ambrosia? She thought not.

However, from her perch in the shade, the Dowager Lady Gold was as cool as a cucumber. Sitting upright, her back two inches away from the back of the patio chair, Ambrosia looked at Ginger with heavily hooded eyes, her soft cheeks rosy from the summer heat. A wrinkled hand rested on the head of the silver-topped walking stick.

"You're just in time for tea, Ginger. You will join me?"

Ginger didn't know why she'd thought she could sneak to her room on the upper floor to tea and a tray of sandwiches brought to her by her discreet maid, Lizzie, before falling into a gentle sleep on her large four-poster bed.

"I'd be delighted," Ginger said. She lowered herself into a nearby chair and took in the beauty of the back garden. Felicia and Charles were mounted on their respective geldings, and Ginger and

Ambrosia watched as they disappeared down the lane.

Ambrosia beamed with delight. "Aren't they a perfect couple? I do hope he soon plans to propose."

"I'm not sure what the hurry is, Grandmother."

Ambrosia stared, her watery-blue eyes flashing with disbelief. "To secure the marriage! Surely, you haven't forgotten the grief Felicia has caused me these last few years with her modern, scandalous ways? The type of men she's attracted—well, I was certain her reputation had been ruined more than once. And now, an *earl*—we could hardly hope for better."

Ginger wasn't so sure.

Lizzie approached with a tray. "We saw you through the window, madam," she said to Ginger. "Mrs. Beasley doubled the portions. Shall I pour the tea?"

Ginger smiled at Lizzie's pixie-like face, her eyes eager to please.

"That would be wonderful," Ginger said. "Thank you, Lizzie."

Ambrosia regaled Ginger with stories about the garden, inserting a grumble over Langley's incompetence—Ginger was thankful the maid had gone inside—and Ginger shared news about how the fashion show was coming along.

Ambrosia *tsked*. "Such a risk to have an event like that outside."

Ginger didn't disagree. After all, it hadn't been her decision. The Lord Mayor and London County Council had wanted to bring people to the park. No doubt, the first time the event got washed out by unrelenting rain would be the end of the spectacle. She encouraged herself by saying, "The men who watch the weather and how it performs say the weather will be splendid."

Ambrosia pursed her lips. "That's nothing more than sorcery."

Interrupted by the sound of Basil's forest-green Austin 7, Ginger smiled as she watched her handsome husband park in the garage beside her Crossley. He switched off the engine and exited with the magnetism of a film star, whilst Scout, their adopted son, jumped out with the enthusiasm of a lad whose voice was changing.

Both wore tennis clothes of white shirts, trousers, and matching V-neck pullovers.

Ginger grinned at the sporty duo, then reached for Basil's hand. He ducked to kiss her on the cheek. "Good afternoon, love."

"Good afternoon to you," Ginger returned with a smile. "So good of you to take the afternoon off to spend with Scout. I hope Superintendent Morris wasn't too disagreeable?"

Basil grinned. "Morris is out of the country."

Ginger chuckled. "When the cat's away . . ."

"Precisely."

Ginger turned to Scout and held his gaze. "How was your lesson?"

"Frightfully fun." Scout pointed to the plate of sandwiches. "May I, Mum?"

Ginger noticed how Ambrosia bristled. The matriarch had never quite latched on to Ginger's desire to adopt what the dowager referred to as a 'street urchin'. After a strongly worded indictment from Ginger, the dowager had agreed to keep her sentiment to herself, at least verbally. Scout was too gracious to notice Ambrosia stiffening every time he entered a room.

"Go and wash first," Ginger said. "Clean clothes, clean face, and clean hands."

Scout's shoulder's slumped. "Yes, madam." But when Ginger's dog, Boss, ran out to greet him, he ran off as cheery as a deer in a meadow in bloom. Basil pulled up one of the chairs.

Like magic, Lizzie arrived with a second tray of

tea and sandwiches, and Ginger marvelled at Mrs. Beasley. To look at the cook, one would be forgiven to assume, based on Mrs. Beasley's girth, that the woman might be slow to move about, but she'd proven to be as quick as any slimmer counterpart.

As Ginger poured Basil's tea, she took in his greying temples and the deepening crow's feet framing his hazel eyes. In her estimation, her husband grew more handsome by the day.

"We stayed to watch a ladies' game," he said.

Ambrosia frowned. "A lady's what?"

"Tennis played by female competitors," Basil explained. "They were surprisingly good."

"In my day, the gentler sex knew their place," Ambrosia said.

"In your day, ladies were constricted by fashion," Ginger said, without pointing out that some Victorian ladies had, indeed, played the sport. "Thankfully, the designs of today are far more liberating."

Ambrosia sniffed. "The frocks have the shape of potato sacks."

Ginger refused to stand down. "And because of that, ladies can play tennis with even more vigour." She turned her focus to Basil. "Did you catch the names of the players? Irene Cummings is on the schedule to model the latest in sportswear at the show."

"Yes, Irene Cummings was there and showed particular prowess. Her partner, Nellie Booth, played well too. I'm thankful that ladies and gentlemen don't play together, or I fear one of us would be dreadfully humiliated."

Pippins, the septuagenarian butler who'd been on staff at Hartigan House for decades—back when Ginger's late father had been the head of house—presented a small silver tray topped with a lone envelope.

"Post for the Dowager Lady Gold," he said.

Ambrosia plucked the envelope off the platter. "Thank you, Pippins." As she read the handwritten name, she blanched.

Concerned, Ginger leaned towards her. "Is everything all right?"

"An old acquaintance is in town. Deborah Harvey, now Deborah, Duchess of Worthington."

Before Ginger could tell Ambrosia that she'd met the Duchess that morning, Ambrosia shifted her chair.

"Langley!" she blustered. "*Langley!*"

The pinched-faced maid scurried outside, her long legs making the venture appear awkward.

"Yes, madam?"

"Take me to my room."

Langley held out her arm, which Ambrosia gripped unceremoniously.

"Oh mercy," Ginger muttered. Lowering her teacup to the table, she said to Basil. "I'm going to see what's troubling her."

Ambrosia could be speedy when she wanted to be, and Ginger could hear the rapid tap, tap, tap of the dowager's walking stick as it struck the black-and-white marble floor of the vast entranceway. Two thick wooden doors facing Mallowan Court were flanked with tall windows letting in the south-facing sunlight. A large chandelier hung from the two-storey vaulted ceiling, and a staircase curved upwards to the upper floor. Ambrosia, with Langley following behind, was already halfway up the stairs.

Ginger felt a little breathless when she reached them.

"Grandmother, what's the matter?"

Ambrosia's cheeks quivered as she shook her head. "Nothing."

Holding on to opposite rails, the two ladies reached the landing simultaneously. "Something has clearly upset you," Ginger pressed. "You know you can confide in me."

Ambrosia gripped the silver-embossed handle of her walking stick with two vein-ridden hands. "Deborah and I were children together. Friends once. But . . ." She pursed her lips and shook her head sharply. "That's all in the past. And if she thinks I'm going to call her 'Your Grace', she'll be sorely disenchanted!"

3

A three-piece brass band entertained the crowd that had gathered for the fashion show. The men, dressed in matching white suits, were in the bandstand in Hyde Park—an octagonal-shaped gazebo with a two-tiered roof topped with a pointed spiral, its roof held secure by eight ornate iron pillars. Together they produced smooth jazz sounds, which most probably could be heard beyond the Serpentine, a long and slender lake that ran through the park like a snake.

Ginger felt the name otherwise unfitting as the area was tremendously beautiful with plenty of leafy, green trees and wide lawns kept mowed by a rather large flock of sheep. Majestic swans floated along the surface of the water. Ginger would always feel fond of the area, as Basil had chosen this park, a romantic spot along the Serpentine, to ask for her hand in marriage.

On this pleasant morning, the skies were blue with puffs of white clouds and the breeze light and refreshing. And, in contrast to the heatwave currently assaulting the east coast of America and Ginger's town of Boston, she couldn't have planned for better weather if she'd overseen it herself!

Chairs set up in rows around the temporarily elevated wooden runway had filled as eager viewers came prepared with picnic baskets and their parasols for shade. Behind the bandstand, several white tents —one for each designer to house their wardrobes and particulars—were arranged in a semicircle, giving each equal access to the runway. British designers Kate Reily and the up-and-coming Bette Perry, Italian designer Elsa Schiaparelli, and French designers Jean Patou and Coco Chanel were among them.

Of those, only Coco Chanel had yet to arrive.

Ginger had decided on a white, sleeveless crepella frock trimmed with blue and red crepe for this occasion. A square collar sporting wide lapels left enough exposed skin to display a matching ruby necklace. A pleated skirt dropped from the waist and was finished with a large wide bow, front and centre, perfect for camouflaging her growing middle. A matching hat with enough brim to shield her eyes from the sun and a pair of red leather pumps finished the outfit.

Ginger searched for Madame Roux, who'd taken on the role of backstage manager, spotting her as she exited one of the tents.

"Madame Roux?"

Madame Roux looked up from her clipboard. "Yes, Mrs. Reed?"

"Is everything going as planned?"

"*Oui, oui*. I've visited all the tents, ensuring each designer and their assistants are aware of the schedule and have the models and their outfits ready." Her lips, thick with dark lipstick, pulled downwards. "Only Mademoiselle Chanel is not here."

Ginger glanced at the last tent on the right. "But her assistant is ready?" she asked hopefully.

"*Oui*. Thank goodness for dependable assistants."

Feathers & Flair had a smaller tent, and Ginger stepped inside. Emma had the outfits numbered and assigned to each model. Felicia had volunteered to perfect the models' finger curls and makeup.

Dorothy assisted Millie, the first of the models walking for Emma, doing up the hooks and eyes on the back of her frock.

"Oh, Mrs. Reed," Emma said, spotting her. "One of the models hasn't come. I already have Millie going twice, but we won't have time to redress our hired model before the next one is set to go. I meant to tell Madame Roux, but she's so busy, I haven't had a chance."

"That's all right," Ginger said. "Madame Roux has enough on her plate. I'll handle it."

Emma's eyes flashed with relief. "Thank you, Mrs. Reed."

Ginger smiled at Felicia. "How about it, Felicia?"

Busy applying rouge circles to the model's cheeks, Felicia asked, "How about what?"

"Will you model for Emma?"

Felicia straightened and stared placidly. "Model? Me?"

"Why not? You're young, beautiful, and, for the most part, graceful."

Felicia laughed. "For the most part?"

Ginger smirked in return. "We can't forget that table-dancing incident and your subsequent tumble, can we?"

Felicia tightened her lips as the girls in the room

held in their giggles. Having made *The Daily News* pages, Felicia's late-night club mishap was hardly a secret.

"That was an unfortunate circumstance, not my usual fare. I can walk that runway as gracefully as the best of them!"

Ginger bit the inside of her lip to keep from laughing. She knew how to bait her younger sister-in-law, and Felicia didn't disappoint.

"I'm glad to hear it," she said. To Emma, she added, "Please help Miss Gold prepare."

Emma nodded. "Yes, madam."

Strolling to the side of the stage, Ginger glanced out at the crowd, spotting her family in the section on one side. Basil sat placidly, attending the show simply to offer his support to Ginger. Ambrosia, shaded by a Victorian-inspired parasol, frowned as her eyes darted about the park. Since receiving the letter from Deborah, Duchess of Worthington, she'd been bristlier than usual and refused to reveal why the message had upset her so. There was a story there, and Ginger suspected—since she'd never heard word of the Duchess before yesterday—that it went back several years.

An empty seat beside Ambrosia was reserved for Felicia, and next to that sat Lord Davenport-Witt.

He leaned in towards Ambrosia, and whatever he said caused Ambrosia to smile.

Ginger approached to relay her news.

"Felicia will be delayed. It turns out we're short a model."

"What does that have to do with Felicia?" Ambrosia said, her brows furrowing. "Surely she's not—"

"She is, Grandmother."

Ambrosia blustered. "But, that's so common—"

"Fashion is for all classes," Ginger said, soothingly. "And she'll be lovely."

Charles chuckled. "I, for one, am delighted. And I have quite a view from here."

On the opposite side of the runway, Ginger saw the tennis players, including Nellie Booth and Irene Cummings—the pretty athlete scheduled to model for Jean Patou's sports collection—and the famous French champion Suzanne Lenglen. She rounded over to them and stretched out her hand to Mademoiselle Lenglen. "Congratulations on your world cup titles," she said. "My son shall be sorry when he hears you were here."

"He's a tennis fan, *oui?*" the tennis champ said.

"Very much so." Turning to Miss Booth and Miss Cummings, she added, "And of yours as well. He and my husband watched your women's doubles game yesterday."

Both athletes smiled, and Miss Cummings said, "Considering she's only returned from Brazil a week ago, Nellie did well. Hardly a chance to rest properly."

As if on cue, Nellie Booth yawned. "Oh dear! Please excuse me."

"Isn't she spoiled?" Miss Cummings smiled, but her eyes flashed with annoyance. "One can hardly feel sorry for her."

"What took you to Brazil, Miss Booth?" Ginger asked with interest. South America was a place she'd never been but would love to visit someday.

"My uncle is a naturalist and invited me along for the adventure. It was timed perfectly during a tennis break."

Ginger smiled. "How wonderful."

"But I'm back now," Miss Booth continued, "and ready to keep my eye on the prize, Wimbledon next year! We'll give Kitty Godfree a run for her money!"

Ginger caught a pained look on Miss Cummings' face before her practised smile returned. "It's wonderful that you came today, despite your recent excursion, Miss Booth," she said. "Miss Cummings, I look forward to seeing you on the runway."

"I'm so nervous," Miss Cummings replied.

Nellie Booth rolled her eyes with unrestrained exaggeration. "You'll be fine."

Ginger thought her a tad rude but chalked it up to journey weariness. Unbidden, Ginger felt a twinge of envy. Despite her adventurous spirit, she had yet to voyage widely. She'd always dreamed of venturing to the southern hemisphere, but now, with a baby on the way, she couldn't see that sort of rigorous travel in her near future.

"Ginger!" Ginger turned at the sound of her name and smiled when she saw her good friends Reverend Oliver Hill and his wife Matilda, pushing a pram as they walked by.

"Hello." Ginger hurried over, eager to get a glimpse of little Margaret. The child, dressed in a white, frilly baby smock and matching bonnet, had grown so much since her birth three months earlier. "Look how chubby her cheeks are!"

Matilda laughed. "She loves to eat. I feel like I'm constantly feeding her." Then, with a note of concern, she added, "How are you, Ginger? You're not overdoing it, are you? I swear, if you start to look ragged, I'll report you to Dr. Longden."

"I promise I'll pace myself."

Ginger's eyes stayed on the baby. After so many

years of not conceiving, she could barely believe that she would have a child soon. "Her hair looks even redder than I remember," Ginger said, noting the fine wisps of copper strands curling onto the baby's forehead.

"Perhaps yours will be the same," Oliver said. His hair was an even darker shade of red than Ginger's.

"Let's hope, shall we?" Ginger checked her watch and excused herself. "I have to be on stage in fifteen minutes. Are you staying to watch?"

"For a little while," Matilda said. "But Margaret gets fussy when she tires."

Ginger waved as she spun away, suddenly knocking into the soft body of Blake Brown, a reporter at *The Daily News*.

"Ah, Mrs. Reed," he said. "Just the lady I was hoping to run into."

Ginger eyed the man suspiciously. A short pencil was tucked behind one ear, shaded by his hat, he held another over an opened notebook. Her path had crossed with Mr. Brown's on a couple of other occasions, and she wondered if he'd actually run into her on purpose.

"I'd be happy to answer your questions regarding the fashion show, but you'll have to walk with me. I'm due on stage in a few minutes and must let the band know it's time to draw it to a close."

"You've got a rather impressive line of designers."

"I wouldn't call that surprising, Mr. Brown. London's fashions have always been forward-thinking."

"Surely not ahead of Paris."

Ginger couldn't deny that Paris was the pinnacle of the fashion world. "We're happy to have France and Italy represented, as well." Ginger slowed long enough to gesture to the filled chairs and the skies. "I'm pleased with the designers' interest, the turnout, and the fine weather."

Keeping pace with Ginger, Mr. Brown continued. "I've confirmed the attendance of Reily, Schiaparelli, and Patou, but Chanel is nowhere to be seen. Could she be avoiding the affair to evade further controversy?"

Ginger highly doubted that. From what she knew of Coco, the lady thrived on controversy.

"You'll have to take that up with her, Mr. Brown."

Ginger reached the stage, pointed at her watch, and signalled to the band leader it was time to stop. The man nodded, and when the piece they were playing ended, the band stepped quietly into the shadows and off the stage.

Ginger picked up the funnel-shaped megaphone.

"Ladies and gentlemen, welcome to London's Summer Fashion Show!"

Ginger saw Basil beaming with pride. Ambrosia, however, looked as if she were about to have a stroke. Following her grandmother's line of sight, Ginger immediately saw the cause of her consternation: directly on the opposite side of the runway was Deborah, Duchess of Worthington, a wide-brimmed hat on her head with an impossibly large feather jutting heavenward from the satin ribbon. She stared across the runway to where Ambrosia sat, a wry smile forming on her face. Whatever was going on between those two ladies had Ginger's curiosity percolating.

Holding the megaphone to her lips, Ginger announced, "Please, take your seats and get comfortable. We are about to begin, and I can tell you that you are going to be very pleased with the show."

The crowd had settled as the designers took to the empty seats reserved for them in the front row.

"Please allow me to introduce to you our designers," Ginger continued. "Monsieur Jean Patou from Paris." Jean Patou had the distinction of employing male models for his men's line and, in particular, his designer tie and cubist cardigan. A handsome man, he removed his bowler hat as he stood, offering a small bow. Polite applause followed.

"Signorina Schiaparelli from Italy."

Elsa Schiaparelli, with her large round eyes, stood as she scanned the crowd before offering a slight curtsy.

The rapid succession of a horn blasting stopped Ginger short. All eyes turned to the two-seater, convertible motorcar driving across the lawn towards the bandstand. An attractive brunette with a heart-shaped face and tantalising dark eyes sat on the edge of the back of the passenger seat, waving a gloved hand as if she were royalty. She held a white parasol over her head, which had a repeating pattern of black connected Cs, a logo that identified the designer's products and, Ginger thought, a brilliant marketing device.

Coco Chanel had arrived.

4

Keeping her composure, Ginger walked toward the flamboyant designer, hearing the other designers' catty comments as she walked by.

"So very like her to make an ostentatious entrance," Monsieur Patou said.

Elsa Schiaparelli spat, "She'll do anything, *anything,* to outshine me!"

The competition between the two ladies was well documented in the fashion world.

Miss Reily was more forgiving. "I find her rather cunning."

Bette Perry, the youngest designer of the group and ripe with hope, sat with wide eyes.

Ginger kept a ready smile, hoping to comfort the loudly murmuring crowd.

"Coco," she said smoothly. "How nice of you to make it."

Coco, unlike anyone else in the crowd, wore strings of black beads with her daring "little black dress", a calf-length black sheath made of chenille. Twirling her parasol, she flashed white, straight teeth.

"Darling, did you not get my telegram?"

"I expected you earlier."

"I am here now."

Coco Chanel's assistant came running. "Mademoiselle, thank goodness," he said in French. "I thought you'd got into a motorcar crash!"

"Oh, Jean-Luc, nothing so dramatic," Coco said with a flick of one glove. "There was a little matter of construction at Piccadilly Circus."

"Yes," Ginger said. "They're putting in a set of traffic lights. I imagine that will make it easier to get to places on time."

Coco Chanel shrugged thin shoulders then instructed her assistant to show her to their tent. Ginger huffed then followed them.

"We're about to start," Ginger said. "I've had my

manager rearrange the schedule so your models will go last."

Coco smiled over her shoulder, and Ginger realised exactly what the designer wanted, the final fanfare. Coco had soared to fame in the last few years, and she wore her importance with panache.

When they reached the door to the tent, Coco lowered her parasol, spinning it for effect. "What do you think, darling?" she said to Ginger. "I am afraid it is the only one in England now, but I am having them made in China for almost nothing. Look at this bamboo stem? Is it not charming?"

"It's quite smart," Ginger admitted.

Coco snapped the parasol closed and propped it in the corner. Her models stood in a row, wide-eyed with obvious awe, each wearing a Chanel original. Coco strutted to each one, not looking any in the eye, only at how her creation was displayed on their bodies.

"It will do," she finally said. Then she said to Ginger. "I thought we were starting?"

"Would you like to be introduced?" Ginger returned. "I've already introduced the others."

Coco's red lips curled in a slow smile. "Of course."

Ginger motioned to the section where the other

designers waited, and Coco, waving to the spectators like Queen Mary, claimed an empty seat, but remained standing. Ginger quieted the crowd and once again held the megaphone to her lips.

"Ladies and gentlemen, Coco Chanel has arrived."

"*Bonjour!*" After a final wave and short curtsy, Coco finally sat.

GINGER GOT the models ready to present the autumn collection, each walking the runway with confidence and poise. The Kate Reily collection would start the line-up then Elsa Schiaparelli, Emma Miller in the middle, followed by Jean Patou, Bette Perry, and finally, Coco Chanel. Regardless of which design house brought them to the event, the mannequins generally modelled something from each designer in rotation. It was the only way to keep the show flowing seamlessly.

However, trouble brewed outside the tent of Feathers & Flair. Ginger had only rounded the tent corner when she witnessed one of the models, Miss Alice White—a tall elfin-type model with platinum-blonde hair styled in neat rows of finger curls—shove her own Millie Tatum in the chest. Ginger gasped as

Millie stepped back to brace herself and nearly tumbled. Having saved herself, she stepped towards Miss White and popped her in the arm with her fist.

"Ladies!" Ginger stated with as much force as polite society allowed. "Please rein yourselves in!"

"Madam?" Millie said, blushing with humiliation.

There wasn't time to allow for explanations. "You are professionals, and I demand that you act like them. Now, Miss White, return to your tent and ready yourself to do your job."

Miss White turned sharply and stomped away, but not without casting a quick snarl in Millie's direction.

"I'm terribly sorry, madam," Millie said. "I shouldn't let her get under my skin. I promise to maintain professionalism from now on."

"I shan't ask what your row was about, but I understand the competitive nature of the modelling industry, and that the stress of such a life could cause one to act out of character."

"Thank you, madam." Millie ducked her head sheepishly and entered the tent.

Inside, Ginger found Madame Roux in control—her clipboard in hand—checking things off. "Ten minutes, Emma," she said before leaving.

Ginger smiled. She'd definitely put the right lady on the job.

Felicia was gazing at herself in the mirror, turning her chin over her shoulder to examine the back of her dress. "It's a delightful frock," she said. The flowing lavender design was sprinkled with sequins, growing denser as they got to the skirt's hem, which sparkled in the light. A sheer scarf in the same shade of purple looped around Felicia's long neck. "Well done, Emma!"

Emma gushed back. "Thank you, Miss Gold."

"And you look stunning in it," Ginger said.

Felicia squealed. "I can't wait to see Charles' face."

Madame Roux returned. "Ladies, time to line up."

Along with Millie and Felicia, two other models strolled out of the tent in single file. Ginger followed, stepping out of line to watch from the far side of the stage.

The crowd hushed the minute the first model, displaying a Kate Reily design, stepped onto the runway, Miss Reily's propensity for fur on display.

Once a model displaying a frock designed by Elsa Schiaparelli hit the runway, Ginger felt herself relax. The show was going swimmingly!

Ginger caught sight of Emma backstage, her face flushed with excitement and anticipation. And the response from the crowd at Emma's creations was very encouraging. Ginger couldn't help but burst with pride at her young protégée's accomplishments.

A model reached the midpoint of the runway, and Felicia stepped out after her. Lacking the seriousness of more seasoned models, Felicia smiled widely, stopping to put a hand on her hip and turning from side to side. When she reached the front of the runway, she caught Charles' eye and made playful overtures to him, hamming it up rather unprofessionally! A low wave of chuckling rippled across the crowd, and Ginger worried that Felicia would ruin things for Emma. Fortunately, a round of models, including Millie, had started their walk wearing Jean Patou's line. With Miss Cummings in the latest tennis wear, some attention lifted off Felicia. All was well until Felicia spun to give Charles one last wink. Somehow, she twisted the heel of her shoe, her knees bent, and the crowd emitted a breathy gasp.

And down she went.

Oh mercy!

5

Before meeting Ginger, Basil Reed had never been aware of the fashion world. Names like Patou, Schiaparelli, and Chanel meant nothing to him.

How things could change in just a few short years. Basil had moved from a moody, job-focused, childless, widower to a married father-of-one with another on the way, and living in a house full of strong Gold ladies and a myriad of staff.

He couldn't have been happier.

A couple of hours spent outdoors watching pretty models strut down a narrow runway, displaying a wardrobe he could acknowledge had some merit, was a small price to pay. But he had to admit, Mademoiselle Chanel's entrance had been a needed spot of diversion and entertainment.

With Ambrosia and her perpetual scowl to one side, and Lord Davenport-Witt, unable to temper his smile, on the other, Basil felt like the brace holding up two sides of a weighted balance. Soon this would all be over, and he could go home and enjoy a drink with his lovely wife who would, though exhausted, regale him with all the drama that was sure to be going on backstage.

As always, his gaze searched for Ginger as she moved about the crowd; she flowed from backstage to stage left, expertly managing everyone involved. He worried about the circles forming under her eyes and how she was prone to overexert herself. He really would have to put his foot down after this. His wife must take proper care of herself in her delicate circumstances. Besides, the loose fashion trends would only hide her condition for so long.

"Hey, old chap," Charles Davenport-Witt said, reaching over to give Basil a nudge in the arm with his fist. "You're looking rather serious."

Basil considered the earl. Ginger had got over her initial distrust of the man but hadn't warmed to him. Charles had spent time in the Great War with

Ginger's first husband, Daniel, but Basil would've thought that would've endeared the man to Ginger. However, Ginger had a past during the war she didn't like to talk about, not even with Basil, though, being the detective he was, he had deduced that his wife had possibly been involved with the British secret service. Ginger would never confirm or deny his suspicions.

"No, not at all," Basil returned. He crossed his legs and strove for a relaxed look. "Just waiting for the excitement to begin."

Ambrosia harrumphed. "I'm about ready to send for Clement to drive me home. This was supposed to start twenty minutes ago!"

Before Ambrosia could execute her threat, Ginger appeared on stage and, after introducing the vivacious Coco Chanel, got the show going.

The train of well-dressed ladies held Basil's attention, but he sat up when Felicia stepped up, a face he recognised.

"There she is!" Charles said, beaming.

Ambrosia pursed her lips, deepening the already ravine-like lines on her face.

Basil chuckled. "Fashion models are respected in high society, Lady Gold," he said.

"Barely a step up from those burlesque clubs,"

was the elder Gold lady's curmudgeonly reply. "But then, how would I know?"

"I can assure you," Basil said, "they are nothing alike."

Ambrosia cast a suspicious scowl, but propriety prevented her from asking how Basil would know.

However, on seeing Charles' happy face, Ambrosia softened. An earl was interested in her granddaughter, and Basil was aware of the many suitors in the past that had not satisfied Ambrosia's standards.

"Very nice, darling!" Charles said as Felicia sashayed towards them.

It was so like her to play things up, and Basil could feel the chill of Ambrosia's disapproval as her eyes darted between Felicia's playful antics and a lady with a large hat and a Cheshire-cat grin on the opposite side of the runway.

Felicia pressed her two index fingers into her rosy cheeks as she leaned in Charles' direction, eliciting vigorous applause from him alone. Then she spun, attempting her return along the runway.

But failing. Dreadfully.

Try as she might, Felicia couldn't regain her balance, and the fall was inevitable. The only question was, would she remain on the runway or fall into the lap of the lady in the hat!

The crowd gasped; Basil and Charles sprang to their feet.

"Felicia!" Charles cried.

The model behind Felicia stopped, her eyes flitting from side to side, uncertainty replacing her trained expressionless face. Then, she grabbed her arm, let out a yell, and went down.

The third model, with a white-blonde bob, looked about with a pinched expression of confusion and appeared to simply lose her footing, falling off the edge of the narrow runway with a wounded cry. Inexplicably, a few moments later, another model went down. This time, there was no cry of pain or attempt at recovery.

Ginger, who'd been watching the spectacle from stage left, stepped toward the final fallen model.

"No!" Basil shouted, "Ginger, stop!"

Leaving an astounded Ambrosia and Charles in his wake, Basil leapt through the chairs, pushing spectators out of the way as he did so.

Someone was attacking the models, and he had to keep Ginger safe, no matter what.

6

Basil reached her, holding her back when her impulse was to see to the fallen model.

"Call the doctor!" Ginger shouted.

"You," Basil said to a stranger next to him, "find a constable and request assistance immediately!"

The young man dropped his hat as he charged away to do Basil's bidding.

"What's happening here? Four models down in a row!" Ginger pointed. "That's Irene Cummings!"

"Wait here," Basil said. He ran to the runway, made the easy jump, and pushed through the gathering crowd. "I'm Chief Inspector Basil Reed. Please step back."

Felicia and Alice White hobbled with mustered

grace near the runway whilst Millie sat upright, clasping her arm. Irene Cummings remained prone but moaned as she tried to lift her head.

Had some malefactor sought to cause havoc by greasing the runway? Yet, there hadn't appeared to be a problem with slippage before now. How could such a prank have been accomplished with no one witnessing the deed?

Curiosity spurred, Ginger could hold herself back no longer. Whatever the danger was, it appeared to be gone now.

"Oh, Ginger!" Felicia, her arm linked with Charles, limped lightly in Ginger's direction. "I'm such a dunce! I've ruined everything!"

"Darling," Ginger said, "I doubt that you can take the blame for the others who fell. Please, just rest." She gave Charles a look. "I trust you'll look after her."

Charles blinked. "Of course."

The spectators had gone from looking scandalised to inconvenienced. As if a round of falling models had been planned purely for their annoyance, murmurs of complaint reached Ginger's ear. More than a few ladies fanned their faces with collapsible, handheld fans, the sharp flicks of their wrists passively criticising the show.

On their feet, hands on hips, the designers bore down on the scene with outraged expressions.

Murmurs reached Ginger's ears. "Did we not all know who they were? This disruption—so terribly unprofessional."

Vexed, Ginger let out a breath then made her way to the runway. The medical man, who'd been hired by the show, was on site and taking charge.

"Let's move the two damaged ladies into the medical tent, shall we?"

Millie walked herself, but it was as if Irene Cummings' legs had turned to jelly. Basil hurried to brace the tennis player under one arm whilst the doctor took her other.

In Ginger's opinion, Miss Cummings certainly didn't look well. "I'll send someone for an ambulance," she said.

Miss Cummings was shifted onto a camp bed where she lay still, dry lips emitting a soft moan.

"What's the matter with her, Doctor?" Ginger asked, concerned.

"I'm not sure. It could be shock."

"Did she hit her head?" Basil asked.

The medical man made a cursory examination. "There appears to be a mark on her neck. A puncture wound of some sort. Whatever it is, she needs to be in hospital. Quickly."

Ginger's pulse jumped at the urgency in the doctor's voice. She turned to Millie, who sat quietly on a chair. "How are you feeling, Millie?"

"Awfully tired. I seem to have scratched my arm, though I can't imagine how."

Ginger wondered the same thing. Millie hadn't misstepped off the runway like Felicia and Miss White had.

Madame Roux entered the tent and announced, "Two ambulances are on their way. Should I send for one for Miss Gold?"

Ginger followed Madame Roux's gaze beyond the tent entrance to where Felicia leaned against Charles, a soft smile on her face.

"No, I think she'll be all right."

When Ginger returned to the stage, she was accosted by the designers.

"The show must go on," Jean Patou declared.

Miss Perry supported the French designer most earnestly. "Ensure the runway is dry and let's get the rest of the girls going before we lose the crowd."

Coco and Elsa shared an air of defeat. "It is already a disaster," Coco said. "It cannot be repaired."

Elsa Schiaparelli nodded reluctantly. "For once, Mademoiselle Chanel and I agree."

A glance at the audience proved that the spectators had indeed grown weary, faces frowning and eyes dulling with boredom. Only propriety and deeply ingrained English manners kept them from leaving en masse. Ginger would be doing everyone a favour by releasing them.

Her eye caught Blake Brown frantically scribbling in his notebook and taking endless photographs. No doubt, he was inwardly rejoicing that what was a rather dry society piece was now a spectacle that would sell papers. Perhaps she could cajole him into leaving unflattering images of her and Felicia out of the story, but that would take leverage that Ginger didn't have.

"Very well," Ginger said. "I'll concede to bringing the event to a close."

Miss Perry huffed as she stormed away. The other designers called for their assistants, but Basil hurried to Ginger's side before anyone could take another step.

"What is it?" Ginger asked, noting her husband's dark and serious look. "I was just about to declare the end of the show and let the people go."

"You must declare the end, but don't release them yet. I'm afraid Miss Cummings has died."

"*What?*" Ginger blinked in disbelief. "From a fall and hitting her head?"

"I don't believe that's what killed her."

"Ah," Ginger said softly. "The wound on her neck."

"Indeed," Basil said gravely. "And until I know the cause, I need everyone to stay put."

"Do you *really* think it could be foul play?" Ginger asked.

"Unless there's such a thing as a murderous hornet," Basil returned. "I just need a bit of time to investigate."

"Of course." Ginger stepped towards the gazebo. "I'll make the necessary announcements."

Ginger's mind whirled as she climbed the steps and picked up the megaphone. Had whatever struck Miss Cummings brushed against Millie as well? Were all the models targeted and the gunman merely a poor shot? No one had heard a gunshot, but perhaps the weapon had been muffled. What kind of pistol used such small bullets? And why on earth would someone bother to shoot her models with that? Unless he had merely meant to cause a disturbance, not for anyone to die.

Ginger scanned the park for trees or outbuildings where such an attacker might conceal themselves from their position on the gazebo. There were no outbuildings in the vicinity, and though there were trees, they were rather far away.

"Ladies and gentlemen," Ginger began. "I'm afraid that we've been forced to bring the show to an abrupt end. I regret to report that we've had a death."

A loud murmur rippled across the crowd, and a few voices shouted the question everyone had on their minds: Who?

"Sadly, Miss Cummings has succumbed to her injuries." Ginger held out a hand to the agitated gathering. "Please! Remain calm. Chief Inspector Basil Reed of Scotland Yard asks that you remain seated for a short while. Officers of the law will take your names and addresses down, and after that, you'll be free to leave."

Respect for the law and those who served within it, or, more likely, unadulterated curiosity, kept the people in their seats and willing to comply.

Ginger joined Basil, who was inspecting the runway.

"Have the constables arrived?" Ginger asked.

"Braxton is here with three others," Basil answered.

A shiny item in the grass caught Ginger's attention. The lawn had uneven patches—flocks of sheep weren't always uniform in the way they chewed the grass—and the object had lodged itself into a tuft. "Basil, there," she said, pointing.

Basil squatted, produced a clean handkerchief from his pocket, and picked up the piece whilst shielding it from those who sat in chairs only ten feet behind him. He showed the item to Ginger.

She gasped and whispered, "A dart?"

Basil swivelled. "There's another." He shifted two paces down the runway and retrieved the one that had landed nearly underneath. Carefully covering both darts with the handkerchief, he placed them in his suit pocket.

Ginger's blood chilled. "Is there a third one?" Had someone targeted Felicia? Had her fall inadvertently saved her life?

Basil reached for a third dart, and his hazel eyes darkened. "There is. Ginger, two of the models were yours."

Ginger conceded to the fact but countered with, "But not the one who died."

"Regardless," Basil said soberly, "I'm afraid we're dealing with murder."

7

In the distance, the shrilling bells of an ambulance could be heard. "Do you think they're in danger?" Ginger asked.

"It's possible," Basil returned. "The men are ready to take names and enquire if anyone spotted anything suspicious. The designers and models are to return to their tents until further notice."

"Chief Inspector!"

The crisp, posh accent of a lady caused Ginger and Basil to turn. Ginger was surprised to see the domineering form of Her Grace the Duchess of Worthington standing there.

"I'm told you're a chief inspector," the Duchess said with presumed authority.

"I am," Basil said. "And you are?"

"I'm Deborah, Duchess of Worthington, and Miss Cummings is my great-niece. I demand to know what happened to Irene. I demand to be taken to her."

"Madam," Ginger started gently. "Miss Cummings has been taken away by ambulance." *Had the Duchess missed her announcement regarding Irene Cummings' demise?* "We're afraid she didn't survive."

"I did hear you the first time, Mrs. Reed," the Duchess said stridently. "I mean to know *what* happened."

"We're doing our best to find out, Your Grace," Basil said. "Would you like a seat? I need to ask you a few questions about your great-niece if you have the fortitude."

"Of course, I have the fortitude." The Duchess accepted the chair, regardless. "It's just a shock. It's not like we were close, though Mary Ann, my sister, and her daughter Joyce, will, of course, be devastated."

"You say you weren't close," Basil started. "Did you know your great-niece would be here this afternoon?"

"I'd heard through the grapevine. My sister is ailing in Hertfordshire and couldn't make it. She is rather proud of her granddaughter—this news might do her in, wretched woman."

"Wretched?" Ginger said, surprised by the Duchess' lack of empathy.

"My sister and I never got on that well, and when I married Theodore, she took it as a personal affront." Her gaze steadied on Ginger. "She wasn't the only one."

"What do you mean?" *Was the lady referring to Ambrosia? That could explain the animosity.*

"Just that all of Chesterton found my rise in rank rather unpalatable."

"I see," Ginger said, understanding. She knew what it was like to marry a title and then lose it again after a second marriage. It was a hard adjustment for all who abided closely by class divisions.

"Do you know of anyone who might've wished Miss Cummings harm?" Basil stepped in closer.

"I'm afraid I'm not aware of her social circle or her daily routines, only that she was beginning to make a name for herself in the sport of tennis. In fact, we only had a brief greeting together before the show. If I hadn't sought her out, she mightn't even have known I was here."

The last sentence was spoken with a trace of bitterness.

"Should the police want to ask you more questions, are you staying in London?" Basil said.

"I can be found at my home," she returned, giving Basil her address in Mayfair.

"Thank you for your time, Your Grace," Basil said.

Ginger added, "Again, our condolences to your family."

Basil offered a hand, which the Duchess accepted, and helped her to her feet. The Duchess of Worthington waved a gloved hand, and immediately, two attendants appeared and escorted the her out of the park.

BASIL TOUCHED Ginger's arm as he whistled at Constable Braxton, who came running. "Stay at Mrs. Reed's side."

"Yes, sir."

Constable Braxton didn't quite catch Ginger's eye, and she felt a little sorry for the officer. He was now counted among many men, "most unsuitable" in Ambrosia's words, who had grown soft on Felicia, only to have their affections eventually slighted. Her sister-in-law *really* did need to settle down, if only to save the hearts of every young man who crossed her path.

"Just until I'm certain the danger has indeed been averted," Basil said a tad sheepishly. He strolled off before Ginger could protest.

"Let us return to my tent, Officer," Ginger said. Though she didn't share her husband's concern for her well-being, she wanted to ensure her staff's safety. Police constables guarded the designers' tents, and conversations could clearly be heard through the thin canvas as Ginger and Constable Braxton walked by.

"Certainly, the danger is passed." This from Jean Patou.

Elsa Schiaparelli snapped, "Are we prisoners now?"

And then Coco Chanel's smooth, accented voice, "Come now, Constable, I only want to look outside. What harm could that do?"

One of Basil's officers responded. "There's been a death, madam. The chief inspector merely wants to get your statement before you go."

Ginger gazed at the front of the stage and was pleased to see that the audience members appeared to be cooperating with the police. While catching Ginger's eye, Charles motioned to Felicia and

Ambrosia and then towards the street, communicating his intention to take the Gold ladies back to Hartigan House. Ginger waved, hoping her response indicated her appreciation.

Now that a life had been lost, the stage, runway, and tents were considered a crime scene, and the police were roping it off. One officer snapped photographs.

The sound of sobbing grabbed Ginger's attention, and she was drawn to a distraught Miss Booth in one of the chairs.

"Mrs. Reed, you were heading to your tent?" Constable Braxton prodded.

"It appears that the police have everything under control, Constable," Ginger said, "and that the danger no longer appears immediate."

Constable Braxton shrugged but stayed close by.

Before Ginger could reach Miss Booth, the woman reached into her handbag and covertly removed a flask. Hiding her face behind one arm, she jerked back as she took a quick drink then deftly returned the flask.

Oh mercy, Ginger thought. *So young to feel the need to keep alcohol on one's person.*

"Miss Booth?" Ginger said when she was in proximity.

Nellie Booth's head popped up at her name. Her eyes, looking very forlorn, were red with tears. Ginger couldn't help but run to the athlete's side and put her arm about her shoulders. The girl's hair had an odd odour, sweet and smoky, perhaps from an earlier encounter with a smoker of exotic cigars. Smoking often did go hand in hand with alcohol consumption.

"You poor thing," Ginger said. "Miss Cummings was your tennis partner. This must be such a horrid shock."

"I just can't believe it, Mrs. Reed. We were meant to play in a tournament this weekend."

"Was she a dear friend?"

"Very."

More tears flooded Nellie's eyes, and Ginger fished through her handbag, producing a clean handkerchief. Nellie received it gratefully.

"Thank you, madam."

"Have you spoken to the police already?" Ginger asked. "Given them your name and address, should they need to speak to you in the future?"

Miss Booth sniffed into the handkerchief as she nodded her head.

"How are you getting home, dear?"

"I took a bus here. I'll find my way to my flat. I'm just so terribly upset."

Ginger caught the eye of Constable Braxton. "Constable, this is Miss Booth, a good friend of the deceased. Can you arrange safe travel arrangements for her back to her flat?"

"Yes, madam,"

"Thank you, Constable," she said.

Miss Booth accepted the handsome constable's arm, and her tears miraculously dried up.

8

Acting as if the murder of her great-niece had been carried out just to upset her evening, the Duchess and her entourage left. Good breeding helped Basil to keep from rolling his eyes. A small token of remorse wouldn't have hurt, but such was the way of many of the elite.

Basil knew this first-hand as his parents, on the lower rung of nobility, still had a way of holding their societal positions over the middle and lower classes' heads—their privilege, a flag waved high above their heads.

Basil's shortened time serving in the Great War had shown him as much. He'd wanted to fight valiantly, do something heroic, but instead he was wounded in a short battle near the beginning of the war, and sent home without a spleen, his tail between his legs. It was how he'd ended up in the police force—his way of doing his bit for the King's service. And when the war had ended, he stayed on, even though he didn't need the pay cheque. Basil found he was good at his job, and it gave him a reason to get up in the morning.

His first marriage to Emelia had been, in many ways, a failure, and over time, he'd made his job his mistress . . .

Until he'd met Ginger.

A lady with a genuine title, the widow of a baron who had lived most of her impressionable years in Boston, had acquired the American disdain for titles and classes. She only started using the title when she'd returned to London after her father had died. After all, British society wasn't wont to let one forget one's place. Ginger had worn it well but never let it, nor the doors it opened, go to her head.

The ease she had interacting with persons of any class inspired Basil more than she knew. That she'd agreed to be his wife even though it meant she'd have to give up her title was no small thing. Basil was humbled by it.

And as for Ginger, he couldn't have loved a soul on earth more, which was why he'd agreed to spend several hours sitting on a hard chair watching women who weren't his wife, traipsing about in new clothes. When Ginger modelled a new outfit for him, it was like he was viewing an angel. Everyone else, especially strangers—no matter how young or beautiful—paled in comparison.

Basil approached the tent of designer Coco Chanel, made a knocking noise on the frame, and pushed the canvas door aside.

The designer who had made that spectacular entrance—or perhaps who had made a spectacle of herself, depending on how one viewed it—sat upright in a chair, legs crossed, the dark seam running down the back of her stockings showing. Smoking a cigarette, she held the ivory holder pinched between two slender fingers.

"Do leave that flap open, darling," the designer said in an authentic French accent. "It is terribly stuffy in here."

Her cigarette smoke didn't help, but he did as requested and tied open the flap.

"I'm Chief Inspector Basil Reed," Basil began.

Mademoiselle Chanel cooed. "Oh, Ginger did say you were delectable. Such a pleasure to see her dessert up close." She ran a tongue over her top lip.

Basil ignored her flirtation, chalking it up to the

way of the French. He cleared his throat. "Mademoiselle, I hope you don't mind if I ask a few questions of you and your entourage."

"Please do. The faster you go, the sooner we shall be dismissed, I expect." She sucked on her cigarette and blew blue smoke into the air. "I don't know how we can help. You certainly can't think that any of us had anything to do with the demise of that poor girl. None of us even knew her."

"Miss Cummings was a rising tennis star," Basil said. "The current champion is French, is she not? That is considered a connection."

"Oh *oui*, my dear Suzanne is spectacular. She has been invited to America, did you know? I have encouraged her to go. The Americans are delightfully barbaric."

"Had you ever met Miss Cummings personally? You or your crew?"

Coco Chanel tapped ash into a tray before extinguishing her cigarette. The resulting smoke spiralled to the tent ceiling and joined a faint cloud there.

"Not I," she said, then waved to the others in the tent. "Any of you?" A round of head-shaking occurred. To her male assistant, she asked specifically. "Have you ever had the pleasure of meeting Miss Cummings, Jean-Luc?"

The assistant responded, "*Non, mademoiselle. Jamais.*"

"There you have it, Chief Inspector," Coco Chanel declared. "We are the *innocent*." She pronounced the final word the French way.

"Bonjour."

Basil turned to the voice of his wife. Ginger never ceased to amaze him with her linguistic abilities. He had always known she was fluent in French, due perhaps to all the time she'd spent in France during the war, but she'd surprised him with her proficiency in German and Russian.

Ginger continued, "*Je suis désolée de vous retarder.*"

Coco waved a hand. "*Ça ne fait rien,*" she said, then finished in English, "It is not like we had any other plans than to be here." Coco pushed off her stool, sashayed to Ginger, kissed her on both cheeks, then eyed Basil. "I suppose it is too soon for the English to kiss in greeting."

"The English are more reserved, as you well know, Coco," Ginger said. "I see you've met my husband."

Coco chuckled. "How unfair that one woman has two beautiful husbands in one life, while others equally deserving, have had none." She returned to her stool. "*C'est la vie.*"

Perhaps the famed French designer had not yet married, but Basil was aware of her ongoing dalliance with a certain married duke.

Ginger smiled at Basil. "Have you found out anything of interest?"

"Not yet, I'm afraid," he said.

"How about you, Coco?" Ginger asked. "Is there anything of note that you can think of that might help?"

Coco's dark-eyed gaze narrowed as she stared at the empty umbrella stand. Frowning deeply, she said, "It appears someone has stolen my distinctive parasol."

How convenient, Basil thought. A hollow bamboo shaft would've made a handy dart blower.

At that moment, Braxton announced his return by clearing his throat. To Basil, he said, "Sir," then he turned to Ginger. "I've delivered Miss Booth into the hands of another officer who will see her home, Mrs. Reed, as you requested."

"Thank you," Ginger said. She raised to her toes to whisper in Basil's ear. "Miss Booth was rather distraught and not at all fit to find her way home on her own. I fear she may have been *intoxicated*."

With a glance at Ginger, Basil acknowledged that further questioning of Miss Booth would be in order.

Coco Chanel cleared her voice. "*Pardonnez-moi*, Chief Inspector. Are we free to go?"

"Yes," Basil returned with a friendly smile, "but please remain in London until further notice."

"Of course," Coco said. "London is my second home."

When he and Braxton stepped outside the tent, the constable gave his report. "All the spectators have had their particulars noted, and, unfortunately, none offered anything of interest. As for the scene, everything is roped off. How long do you want the stage set-up to remain, sir?"

"The stage and tents should stay as-is for now," Basil answered. "We can re-examine with fresh eyes in the morning."

"Yes, sir," Braxton said before turning away.

After a long exhale, Basil glanced at his wife and said, "I can't imagine what more we can find here."

"I agree," Ginger said. "All the witnesses are gone, the body taken to the mortuary, and the darts entered into evidence, I presume."

"You presume correctly."

Ginger looped her arm through his. "When do you think the inquest will be held?"

"Hopefully, as soon as possible. I don't know how long we can compel our out-of-town witnesses to remain in London."

Except for a group of nosy parkers, the police had cleared and contained the area.

Noting the fatigue in Ginger's eyes, Basil felt a wave of tenderness. "Let me take you home, love. You look rather exhausted."

"I am," Ginger agreed.

As they approached the street, the driver of a black taxicab opened the back passenger door. A young lady with an elfin flair got inside.

"That's Alice White," Ginger said. "She and Millie got into a terrible row before the show started." She waved a gloved hand in the air. "Miss White!"

Either Miss White didn't see them or pretended not to, sliding into the back seat without looking back. Basil whistled, but constant noise from the city kept the taxi driver's attention. Before either Basil or Ginger could stop the model, the taxicab drove away.

"I saw her fall off the runway seconds after Millie, but she appeared uninjured. Only her pride ruffled."

"We should interview her," Basil said.

"She lives near St. George's Church," Ginger said. "In fact, I've seen her in attendance there on occasion. Oliver and Matilda would know how to contact her."

Basil adjusted his hat. "Splendid. I'd like to know exactly what precipitated her fall."

9

The next morning after breakfast, Ginger set Scout up with his tutor, then she persuaded Felicia to accompany her to her office of Lady Gold Investigations. Most mornings, she dropped in to check on Madame Roux and the affairs at Feathers & Flair, but with the murder the day before, she felt it prudent to drop Felicia at her investigation office first. *Someone should be there*, she thought, *to answer the telephone and greet anyone who might walk in off the street.*

Formerly a shoe repair shop, Ginger had had the space cleaned and redecorated with an art deco flair. Cream wallpaper printed with gold fans covered the walls, large swathes of carpeting hid the blemished wooden floor underneath, and high windows captured the daylight.

Felicia flopped onto the chair behind her desk—a smaller version of Ginger's own—and held fingers over her mouth as she unsuccessfully tried to squelch a yawn. "Dragging me out of bed so early this morning, Ginger, was rather unnecessary, don't you think?" Felicia complained.

"The early bird catches the worm." Ginger unclipped Boss' leash, and the small dog promptly went to the wicker basket behind Ginger's chair and curled into a ball.

Ginger laughed. "I see Boss shares your sentiments."

Felicia grumbled, "I'm tired enough to drink a cup of coffee. Shall I make you some?"

"Good idea."

Pushing away from her desk, Felicia stumbled out of the office, down a narrow corridor, and through an opened kitchen door. Ginger noticed Felicia's rumpled frock and suspected more was going on with her sister-in-law than a little lost sleep.

Picking up a pencil, Ginger stared at the notepad on the top of her desk, a new page waiting.

"Let's recap, shall we, Boss?" Ginger said. In neat

cursive script, she wrote on the top of the page: The Death of Irene Cummings.

"Everything was running smoothly until twelve minutes past three when Felicia lost her balance at the end of the runway." Concerned the show was running late, Ginger had just glanced at her watch. She marked the page with a dash and wrote: 3:12—Felicia slips.

"Within seconds, Millie goes down, followed by Alice White."

As if complaining about his nap being interrupted, Boss moaned.

Ginger smiled at her pet then jotted, 3:13—Millie and Alice fall.

After a rumble of shock had blanketed the audience, Irene Cummings fell. Jotting in her notes, Ginger added: 3:14—Miss Cummings falls.

Felicia returned with a tray, and Ginger, who'd recently found she'd developed a rather dangerous sweet tooth, helped herself to cream and sugar then took a sip. "Not bad," she said. "I do believe you've been making this deplorable coffee for some time."

Felicia lifted a shoulder but didn't deny the charge. "One does what one must when under a deadline."

Felicia wrote mystery novels for a London

publisher under the name of Frank Gold, more for the prestige than the money. Even though she used a *nom de plume*, Felicia made sure that everyone she was acquainted with knew she was the author. She nodded to Ginger's notepad. "What are you doing?"

"Reviewing yesterday's events. I haven't got far. Perhaps you can help me."

"I'll try."

Ginger read out her notations.

"Charles had assisted me off the stage," Felicia said. "I was flummoxed when I saw that two other girls had fallen. At first, I thought someone had played an awful prank, greasing the runway so that the models would slip."

"Had you found the runway to be slippery?" Ginger asked. She'd examined the runway but had seen nothing suspicious.

"Not particularly. I'm afraid my tumble can only be attributed to bad posture."

"So, you fell, then Millie, then Alice . . ."

"Was Alice wounded?" Felicia asked. "Like Millie?"

"She didn't appear to be. Millie scratched her arm. Possibly a result of her stumble." *Or had she been nicked by one of the other two darts Basil had found under the runway?*

"Didn't the two of them have a row?" Felicia asked.

"Yes, I witnessed it myself. I didn't see Alice again until Basil and I were leaving. She drove off in a taxicab before I could enquire further."

"So curious that she wasn't injured," Felicia said.

"We can be thankful she wasn't. But it makes me wonder . . ."

"What?"

"If Irene was the intended target. Perhaps the killer was just a poor shot."

"Oh. Do you think it was meant for Alice?"

"Who's to know? Any one of the fallen could've been the main target."

Felicia's hand fell to her chest. "Surely, not me?"

"It's not likely," Ginger said reassuringly. "Your fall was most probably a fluke of timing, that's all."

"I most definitely turned my ankle," Felicia said. "That blunder belongs to me alone."

Ginger reached for the black cradle-receiver, dialled the number, and asked the operator to connect her to the vicarage at St. George's Church. Matilda soon gave her the information she needed, and after a round of pleasantries, she said goodbye.

"I'll come along if you don't mind," Felicia said softly. "I'd like the diversion."

Ginger tilted her head and squinted. "I like to think I'm the perceptive type, Felicia."

"Yes?"

"Is everything all right? You seem a little ill at ease. How are you and Charles?"

"Ginger! Sometimes I feel like I must wear a bag over my head to keep things from you." Felicia looked away as her lip quivered.

Boss, who'd awakened and was busy scratching himself with his hind leg, sensed her sadness and trotted to her side, nudging her hand with his wet nose.

"Oh, Boss." Felicia scrubbed his ears. "You're so much like your mistress."

"He wants to comfort you," Ginger said. "As do I. You can confide in me, Felicia. I'm on your side."

"I know that." Felicia sighed then sipped her coffee. "He's cross with me."

"Why?"

"Because I started sulking when he told me he was going to France again—it's the third time this month! And when he still didn't ask me along, I accused him of having an assignation."

Ginger didn't think that was beyond possibility but kept her opinions to herself. "What did he say?"

"That I was being a silly child. How could he

reference our age difference? It's never once come up in all the weeks that we've been associating. And now, after my tantrum, I can't say that he's wrong!"

Felicia dug in her desk drawer, produced a handkerchief, and sobbed. "I don't know if this is clean, and I don't care!"

Ginger hoisted herself from her chair. She was over halfway through her pregnancy and felt the weight and awkwardness of her growing form.

"Dear Felicia," she said as she rubbed her sister-in-law's back. "I believe Charles cares for you very much, and if he has to go to France, it's for a good reason."

"I want to believe you, but you know what French girls are like. They have no scruples at all."

The bell above the door rang. Felicia grabbed her handbag and hurried away, no doubt to the water closet down the hall to repair her make-up.

"Bonjour!" a female voice called.

Speaking of French girls, Ginger thought.

Coco Chanel swept into the office.

After critically assessing the decor of Lady Gold Investigations, Coco mewed, "Ginger, darling, your butler told me I could find you here."

"Would you like a seat?" Ginger offered,

motioning to the two empty curved-back chairs facing her desk.

"*Merci*," Coco said. She wore a pleated skirt and a blouse of colourful horizontal stripes. To this ensemble, a loose summer, fine-knit cardigan was added—a silk rose pinned to the right shoulder. Along with Coco's signature multi-strands of white beads, a feminine version of the trilby was positioned just so on her head.

"I see I missed coffee time."

"Would you like one?" Ginger asked. "We can make more."

"Is it strong like the Europeans make it? I loathe the watered-down *dishwater* they call coffee here in England."

"We can make it that way," Ginger said.

Felicia returned to the main room, her face tidy and her expression bland. "Hello, Mademoiselle Chanel," she said.

"Good morning, Miss Gold."

"Felicia?" Ginger started. "Would you mind preparing coffee for our guest? Please prepare it extra strong."

Felicia grimaced in a manner that suggested she did, in fact, mind but went about her duty as Ginger's assistant, anyway.

Once Felicia was out of sight, Ginger probed, "I suspect you're not here for a simple visit."

After a little shoulder lift, Coco admitted it. "I am here on business. I fear I might be in the sights of your Scotland Yard."

"You were rather brassy yesterday."

"Yes, well, I did not think for a moment that I might be a suspect."

"But today?"

"I had a chance to sleep on it and see where I might have been *un peu désinvolte*."

Ginger agreed that Coco had been too flippant regarding the seriousness of the crime.

"Your husband and his constable came to my house. Though my maid shooed them away, they did not leave until after learning that Jean-Luc was situated at the Ritz." She narrowed challenging, dark eyes. "I fear they are on the prowl."

"I see." Ginger tented her fingertips. "What do you want from me?"

"You are an investigator, are you not?"

"I look into matters of concern to private citizens."

"*Exactement*. I have a matter of concern. I would like you to prove my innocence."

Though feeling astonished, Ginger kept her expression blank. Felicia entered with another tray.

"Cream and sugar, mademoiselle?"

"Oui, *s'il vous plaît*."

"Felicia . . ." Ginger started. "Mademoiselle Chanel and I need a moment alone. Would you mind checking in with Madame Roux and the girls? Let them know I shall be there soon to see how they are."

Felicia grimaced again, and Ginger wrote her sister-in-law's poor mood off on troubling matters of the heart.

"Cheery *fille*," Coco said after Felicia had left.

Ginger deflected by saying, "We're all rather upset about poor Irene Cummings."

Coco sipped her coffee, frowned, but politely did not comment. She placed her cup down on Ginger's desk. "A terrible affair. One that I had no part in."

"The police suspect your parasol may have been used to perpetrate the crime."

"*Mon Dieu!* I am being framed, Ginger. I need your help."

"I'm not the right person for the job, Coco. You do recall that my husband is a chief inspector at Scotland Yard and is working on this case. If I represent you, he and I will be working on opposite sides."

"From my perspective, I get two deals for one. He will tell you what he knows, and you can use it to prove my innocence."

Ginger leaned back in her chair and narrowed her eyes. *Such impertinence!* Boss, sensing her displeasure, emitted a low growl.

"I can't do it," she said.

Coco smirked. "But you owe me. Or have you forgotten?"

Ginger swallowed back the bile that had formed in her throat. Of course, she hadn't forgotten. While on assignment in France during the Great War, Coco Chanel had recognised her. Ginger had always thought the possibility was there and avoided Americans as a precaution. She'd never thought Coco Chanel, not yet famous, would be the one in the position to blow her cover.

As bad luck would have it, Coco had been in Boston in the summer of 1913 and had read about Ginger's marriage to Daniel, Lord Gold. The daughter of a prestigious and wealthy Bostonian marrying into the British peerage was big societal news. Their wedding photo had made the papers, and as serendipity would have it, Ginger and Coco had attended the same theatre performance. Ginger didn't see Coco, but Coco had seen her.

And as she liked to remind Ginger, Coco never forgot a face.

Ginger begged Coco not to give her ruse as Antoinette LaFleur away, and Coco had promised, a promise she'd kept as far as Ginger knew. Englishman Arthur Capel ran top-secret intelligence missions between London and Paris during the Great War, and Ginger had been involved in one of them.

Coco and Arthur—commonly called "Boy"—had been involved in an affair during those years, right until Arthur's death a year after the end of the war, and Ginger didn't know how much Coco knew.

As if reading her mind, Coco said, "The French have no obligation to keep the Official Secrets Act of the English. I do it out of the kindness of my heart and with a fondness for our friendship."

Ginger huffed. "I highly doubt that, Coco, but you've got me on a knife's edge. I'll do my best to prove your innocence. However, if I discover you're *not* innocent, I won't keep that from the police, Secrets Act or not."

"Fair enough, *ma chérie*," Coco said. She paused, and as if to offer an olive branch added, "Your young seamstress, Miss Miller. I was slightly intrigued by her designs."

Slightly intrigued.

Ginger bit her lip to prevent a grin. "I'll pass on your praise. Emma will be thrilled."

"Of course," Coco returned, standing. "You know where to find me."

"I do."

After watching her new client leave, Ginger patted her leg and called for Boss. "Oh, Bossy," she said as she lifted him into a snuggle. "I hope I haven't just climbed into bed with the devil."

10

Scotland Yard was a second home to Basil. He spent as much time there as he did at Hartigan House with his family, and before Ginger had come into his life, he was at the Yard more than not. Though his office was little more than a grandiose storage room, he had a desk, chair, and several full filing boxes. And, a new addition in the last year, a black telephone with a cradle handpiece.

After setting his briefcase on the desk, he removed his summer suit jacket and straw trilby hat and hung them on the rack in the corner. He lowered himself into his chair, anticipating the squeak that refused to go away despite repeated oiling, and snapped the hinges of his briefcase. Inside were his notes regarding the crime scene from the day before.

Braxton ducked inside. "Tea, sir?"

"That would be splendid," Basil said. "Oh, do you know if the photographs from the crime scene have been developed?"

"I'll check for you, sir."

"Thank you."

Does the forensic laboratory have any reports, particularly regarding the substance on the dart that caused Miss Cummings' death? Anxious for answers, he knew he must practise more patience before hearing from the technicians or the pathologist.

Taking out his notepad, he cleared a space on his desk, opened it up, and reviewed his notes.

~The deceased had a puncture wound in her neck

~ Three darts found on the scene likely caused the neck wound

~ Miss Chanel wasn't in her seat at the time of the victim's demise

~ Miss Chanel's assistant, Jean-Luc Marchand, also away from his post

~Miss Chanel's parasol missing—murder weapon?

Braxton arrived with the tea. "I've already added milk and sugar, sir."

Basil lifted the saucer and teacup, raised the cup

to his lips, and blew carefully before sipping. "Splendid, Braxton, thank you."

A manilla envelope was tucked under Braxton's arm. He handed it to Basil. "The photographs, sir."

"Righto. Do have a seat, Braxton."

"Yes, sir."

As Basil opened the envelope and let the contents spill onto his desk, Braxton shifted nervously in his seat. "Uh, sir, how is the family?"

Basil stilled, lifting his gaze to the constable, a pleasant-looking young man. He knew Brian Braxton wasn't interested in the whole of his family, per se, but rather, a particular member. Felicia, as she was wont to do, had been teasingly playful with his constable's heart, and he, like other unfortunate members of his sex, had been left to pine when Felicia had lost interest. He hoped to the heavens she and Charles Davenport-Witt would soon announce an engagement if only to spare the hearts of the available young men of London.

"They are well, thank you. Now, let's look at these, shall we?"

Basil spread the stack of glossy black-and-white photos across his desk. Having been taken after the fact, most shots showed an empty runway, trampled lawn, empty chairs, and an abandoned gazebo.

"What do you see, Constable?"

Braxton rubbed his chin. "Hyde Park, sir."

"Anything beyond the obvious?"

The constable wrinkled his nose. "Should there be, sir?"

That was the million-pound question. Basil scoured the photographs again, frustrated by the possibility he was missing something. If something was staring him in the face, he was staring right back without seeing a clue. Blowing out a frustrated breath, he scooped up the photos, returned them to the envelope, and secured the envelope in his briefcase.

"I think it's time to talk, once again, to our friend, Miss Chanel."

11

Being out of luck at the townhouse belonging to Miss Chanel, Basil determined a conversation with her assistant would be the next best thing. Jean-Luc Marchand had a room at the Ritz—*rather nice for a person who dresses models for a living,* Basil thought. It was an indicator not of how well Monsieur Marchand was doing, but of how successful Coco Chanel had become.

Braxton drove the black police motorcar towards Piccadilly, bringing the machine to a stop at the kerb in front of the Franco-American-designed luxury hotel.

Inside, they were immediately greeted by a liveried doorman who, on seeing Braxton's police uniform, directed them down the bright and airy gallery to the front desk.

An attendant glanced up from his work and smiled at Basil. "Good day, sirs," he said, greeting them politely. "Welcome to the Ritz. What can I do for you today?"

"Hello, good man," Basil said. "I'm Chief Inspector Basil Reed from Scotland Yard. I understand a Monsieur Marchand is a guest here. Perhaps he is being visited by Mademoiselle Chanel?"

At the clerk's stunned expression, he added, "Just a few questions regarding an event at the fashion show yesterday. They're not in trouble with the police, I assure you."

Not yet, anyway.

"Oh, I did hear about the trouble in Hyde Park," the clerk said. "Dreadful affair. But I'm afraid Mademoiselle Chanel has not been to the Ritz today."

Basil held on to his disappointment.

"But if it's Mr. Marchand you're after, he's in the Palm Court."

"Thank you." Basil tipped his hat.

The Palm Court, a popular tea and coffee room in London, had been visited by Basil on several occasions, and not all of them due to his job. With a palette of white, off-white, cream, and gold, the bright and cheery room was dotted with potted palm plants, giving it a Mediterranean feel, and was clearly the reason for the room's name.

Monsieur Marchand wore a stylish scarf around his long neck and a black beret sat on the empty seat beside him. His eyes rolled to the side when he spotted Basil and Braxton walk his way.

"Bonjour," he said politely.

"Good day, Monsieur Marchand," Basil returned. "Might we have a moment?"

"*Certainement.*" He flicked a wrist towards the empty chairs. "Make yourselves comfortable."

Basil and Braxton took a seat. A waiter asked if they would like to order, but Basil said they wouldn't be staying long. Monsieur Marchand requested another coffee.

"We had hoped to find Mademoiselle Chanel with you," Basil said. "Do you happen to know where she is today?"

"Me? *Non.* Mademoiselle is like *un oiseau exotique,* an exotic bird that flies about—with no regard for the other birds."

Basil continued the questioning as Braxton took notes.

"How long have the two of you been acquainted?"

"Ah, it feels like forever. At least a decade. She took me under her wing, and I have not dared to leave it."

"Why is that?" Basil asked. Mademoiselle Chanel had a pull on her assistant. *Enough that he would do her bidding? Even if it was to commit murder?*

"Because she is the best. To move to another house would be a demotion!"

"Last night, you told me that you left your position at the tent to visit the facilities. Is it common for a designer's assistant to leave their tent unmanned?"

"It is not like I was chained to the front door, Chief Inspector. All the assistants hover between their tents and the stage during these events. Everyone is aware of the others' designs, and one would not mistake one's tent for another. We don't expect foul play as a matter of course."

"Indeed. And you never saw anyone behind the stage that gave you pause? Someone who perhaps acted lost?"

Jean-Luc shook his head. "Non, monsieur. When the girls started falling, I was filled with shock. I thought perhaps the runway had been weakly made, and the weight of all four models on it at the same time had caused it to buckle. Never in my wildest imagination did I think for a second that it was a villainous affair."

Jean-Luc removed a cigarette case and matchbox from his blazer pocket and lit a hand-rolled cigarette with flair. Crossing his legs at the knees, he blew a cloud of smoke above their heads. "Is there anything else, messieurs?"

Basil reluctantly pushed away. "You'll contact Scotland Yard if you think of anything that could help us solve this crime?"

"Of course. *Au revoir.*"

12

Conveniently, Ginger's Regent Street dress shop was just around the corner from her investigation office, and a short walk for Boss as she led him on his leash. Her strides were short and clipped as energy burst like gunshots from her emotions towards her new client. She felt manipulated and coerced. There was nothing she could do now since she'd begrudgingly agreed to take Coco Chanel on, except to solve this case and prove her innocence.

The debate Ginger was now destined to have with Basil would be one in which she'd be forced to remain vague. She hated the thought of it.

Regent Street was a bustling affair. Since the end of the Great War, more motor vehicles filled the street, nearly outnumbering the horse-drawn carts and carriages. It wouldn't be long before horses wouldn't be found amongst vehicle traffic, and the poor lads who collected horse droppings for a living would need a new line of work.

In this prime shopping district, high-fashioned ladies with shopping packages in their arms and smiles on their faces strolled the pavements. It was another change that had occurred since the war. During the early years after the turn of the century, the males in the pedestrian population had greatly outnumbered the females. Men dominated business, and even now, some resented how ladies like Ginger had taken over some of their ranks.

Reaching the front door of her shop, Ginger paused to admire the fashions displayed on the window mannequins. The bell rang as she stepped inside, and she paused briefly to swoop Boss up before he could make paw prints on the marble floor. Seeing Ginger enter with her pet, Madame Roux hurried over with a cloth to wipe Boss' dirty paws.

"Thank you, Madame Roux," Ginger said.

Boss, familiar with the routine, waited patiently as each paw was attended to. Once set on the floor, Boss trotted across it, nails clicking like typewriter keys, as he headed to the velvet curtain at the back, nudged his nose through the seam, and headed towards his food.

Ginger pulled off her white gloves, one finger at a time. "Where's Felicia?" She was surprised that her sister-in-law wasn't lounging lazily on the stool behind the sales counter.

"Miss Gold is out the back with Emma and Millie."

"Millie's here?" Ginger didn't hold in her surprise. "Her injury didn't prevent her?" Only a nick of the flesh, the emotional toll from the experience was most certainly higher.

"She said she couldn't afford to take a day off," Madame Roux began, "but, if you don't mind my saying, it's rather hard to dress a model with a swatch of gauze taped to her arm. So many of the gowns are sleeveless."

The front bell announced two new customers. Madame Roux, with thick lipstick and wide, painted eyes, smiled as she welcomed them.

Ginger offered her greeting, leaving them in Madame Roux's capable hands. She crossed the room to the back wall and slipped through the velvet curtain. Felicia and Emma stared with worry in their eyes.

"Oh, Ginger," Felicia said. "Thank goodness you're here. Millie nearly fainted."

The slender model looked paler than usual, and Ginger could see moisture sprouting on her brow.

"Might I have a look?"

Millie carefully pulled back the gauze. Though the tearing of the skin was slight, it was red as if infected.

"Have you had this looked at?" Ginger asked.

"It's just a nick."

"Yes, but whatever struck you might've been dirty. I fear it appears infected. Best to get it looked at. A stitch in time saves nine."

Millie pressed the gauze back in place.

"Yes, madam. I'll seek out a doctor."

"You shouldn't have come to work today. You must rest and give your body time to heal."

"I can't miss work, madam." The poor girl's voice came as a whisper. Ginger knew that Millie came from a middle-class family and not from the poorer population of London.

"What is it, Millie?" she asked. "Are you in trouble?"

Millie's eyes darted from Ginger to Felicia and then Emma behind her. Ginger turned to them. "I believe Madame Roux and Dorothy, who I assume is upstairs, could use your assistance."

"Yes, madam," Emma said, hurrying out.

Felicia flashed a look that Ginger knew well—she'd want to be filled in later—but did as she was bid.

"Let me make a pot of tea," Ginger said. They had teamaking facilities in the corner, and Ginger set a kettle of water on the gas ring. Then, taking a chair, she leaned in and asked kindly, "What kind of trouble are you in? Please, you can confide in me. Perhaps I can help."

"It's just so—" Millie broke into sobs, and Ginger found a clean handkerchief to give to her. Millie carefully dabbed under her eyes but failed to prevent the black mascara from smearing.

"It's embarrassing, madam. I acted, er, indiscreetly, and now my nemesis is threatening to go to the papers."

"And this revelation would be damaging to your reputation," Ginger said, understanding.

"Not only mine but—"

"His?" Ginger ventured.

"Yes."

"Does Alice White have something to do with your distress?"

Millie's eyes went wide. "Why do you say that?"

"You haven't forgotten that awful row you had at the fashion show, have you?"

"Oh, *that*. Alice is annoying but harmless. We were fighting over a specific frock we both wanted to wear. Silly, really."

The kettle whistled, and Ginger proceeded to make tea.

"You shouldn't be waiting on the likes of me," Millie said.

"Oh, pish-posh." Ginger handed Millie the saucer and teacup. "Can you manage this with your bad arm?"

"Fortunately, it's my left, and I'm right-handed."

"I added extra sugar," Ginger said. "You need your strength."

"Thank you, madam."

Ginger sipped her tea, then set the cup and saucer carefully on her lap. "I can assure you, Millie, that everything you tell me shall be kept in my confidence unless, of course, the information is needed to solve a crime. Even then, I'll do my best to keep your name out of it."

"Thank you, madam. Your reputation for discretion in London is renowned. I live alone in my bedsit. I'm afraid. I can't think of a reason why someone would want to kill me, but I can't think of why Irene was attacked either. It's the other reason I came to work."

"Well, it does no good to jump to any conclusions. However, you're in luck. I just happen to know fellows in the police who'd be happy to watch over your safety." She patted Millie's knee. "Now, who's the man in question?"

Millie inhaled deeply as if the coming confession injured her physically. "It wasn't anything, just a kiss, and a chaste one at that, but an unscrupulous person snapped a photograph and is prepared to lie about the extent of it. Some people will do anything for an extra shilling!"

"Who took the photograph?"

"One of those unscrupulous newspaper men who don't care about an innocent lady's reputation, madam."

Ginger sipped her tea, then asked, "Who kissed you, Millie?"

"Monsieur Patou."

"Jean Patou, the designer?"

"Yes."

Ginger thought the threat ambiguous because Monsieur Patou had never been seen in public with a romantic relationship, and rumours in the fashion world would suggest he had no natural interest in women.

But it was a line worth investigating. Perhaps a competitor of Monsieur Patou's had hoped to tarnish his reputation.

Unwelcome, Coco Chanel—the most competitive lady Ginger knew—popped into her mind.

"Can you think of anyone who'd wish you serious harm?" Ginger asked.

Millie shook her head. "That's just it, madam. I live a fairly boring life. I'm not very competitive by nature, generally. I only model because God gave me a shape and a look that suits the work. I'm just trying to make a living. I've done nothing and have nothing worth killing me over." She lifted her left arm, then winced.

"You must see a doctor then go home and rest," Ginger said. "I'll see to your wages for the rest of the day and pay for your taxicab. I can ensure that a constable is there to meet you and watch over your door."

Constable Braxton came to mind. After being toyed with so casually by Felicia, the heart-crushed officer could use the diversion of another pretty girl. Millie was just the sort of girl to heal the constable's heart for good.

13

When Ginger rang Scotland Yard, she was told that Basil was out and hadn't returned, although Constable Braxton had just walked in. When Ginger reported Millie's need, Constable Braxton, as Ginger had suspected, was eager to assist.

Despite Millie's protestations, Ginger wasn't quite ready to let Alice White off the hook. The row over outfit choice might've been harmless from Millie's point of view, but Miss White might've taken it far more seriously. Competition between models was even more feverish than between designers, and if Miss White knew about Millie's association with Jean Patou, she might've felt Millie was being favoured.

After dialling up the operator, she ascertained the address of Miss White's flat. Ginger stared at Boss, who'd entered the room with the hope of adventure in his brown eyes. "Do you want to go for a ride, Bossy?"

Boss' stubby tail wagged so rapidly it seemed almost to blur.

"Let's go, then, shall we?" Ginger collected her handbag, put on her gloves and hat, and attached Boss to his leash.

The drive, particularly the borough of Covent Garden to the City of London, was pleasant enough. The summer warmth allowed for a breezy drive with the windows down. Boss jutted his nose out of the window, delighted with the wind in his face—a wide mouth and long tongue proof of his enjoyment.

Ginger had grown used to the city's smells, which were on the rather odorous scale, the heat exacerbating the scent of horse and dung mixed with petrol exhaust. It was especially bad on foggy days—London was infamous for its propensity for smog—but on this day, the clouds were high and the sun bright.

As Ginger reached the area of St. Paul's Cathedral, an iconic structure with a world-famous dome that simply outsized everything else around it, she recognised the block of flats. She'd had reason to visit former tenants back when Felicia had wanted to be a theatre performer.

With Boss under one arm, Ginger entered the building. A strong smell of cigarette smoke and a mildly rancid scent of cooking grease assaulted her senses. Climbing the stairs, she found the door she was looking for and knocked, hoping that serendipity would find the model at home. When no answer came, Ginger knocked again. Moments later, she heard the shuffling of footsteps towards the door. Boss heard it too and cocked his head, ears tall, to the sound.

The door opened two inches, stopped by a chain fastening it to the frame. Alice, hair pressed up on one side and make-up smudged, narrowed her eyes as if the light hurt them.

"Mrs. Reed?" she said, her voice scratchy.

"I'm dreadfully sorry," Ginger said. "Did I get you out of bed?"

"It's all right." Alice unhooked the chain. "I'm not feeling too well."

Ginger had a pretty good notion Miss White's malady had something to do with the empty vodka bottle on the table and the two empty glasses.

"You don't mind if my little dog joins us, do you?" Ginger said.

Miss White blinked at Boss as if she hadn't noticed him before that moment. "Fine by me, but if he makes a mess..."

The flat was in disarray, and Ginger doubted that Boss could make it much worse. "I assure you, he's very well trained."

Miss White lifted the clothing draped over the arm of one chair for Ginger's benefit. "I hope you're not expecting tea," she said. "I'm completely out."

Ginger didn't know if the model was out of tea or simply not prepared to play hostess, but it didn't matter to her. She didn't plan on staying long.

"That's quite all right."

Alice pushed a pile of laundry to one end of the sofa and curled her petite form upon the other. Her slender hand flew to her face to cover a yawn.

"I'll get right to it," Ginger said. "I'm investigating the death of Miss Irene Cummings."

"Such a blasted shame," Miss White said.

"Yes, it is," Ginger agreed, "and I'm circling back to the people who knew her to see if I can find any leads."

"All right. Ask away."

"How well did you know Irene?"

"Not at all. She's not a real model, as you know. Jean Patou wanted an athlete to demonstrate his sportswear. Guess he thought the line would be taken more seriously by the sports world that way."

"Not a bad marketing ploy," Ginger agreed. "Are you a fan of tennis?"

Miss White shook her head then reached for her eyes as if she immediately regretted the sharp movement. "Couldn't swing a racquet to save my life," she muttered.

"What about the other models? How well do you know them?"

"We all know each other. The fashion world isn't that big, but I suspect that you know that, Mrs. Reed, in your line of work."

"Yes. You're aware that Millie Tatum works in my shop."

"Lucky her."

Ginger noted the model's facetious tone.

"I take it the two of you aren't great friends."

"See? This is why they say you're a terrific detective."

Ginger ignored the sarcastic remark. "Tell me about your row with Miss Tatum?"

Miss White let out a loud, grievous sigh. "Millie and I always row. That's nothing new. She always wants the best outfits, and I've had enough of her trying to climb ahead of me. I've been modelling longer, you know? I should get first choice. Millie's a conniving, greedy, selfish cow who only cares about herself."

Ginger could barely hold in her shock at Miss White's sharp words. Her description of Millie didn't sound like anything Ginger had seen. In fact, Miss White's description more aptly fit herself.

"Where were you when Millie and Miss Cummings were struck down?"

Miss White stared incredulously. "At the show."

"I mean precisely. I understand you fell off the runway. Where did you go then? Backstage? To one of the tents?"

"I was backstage."

"Did anyone see you?"

"Do you honestly think I'm guilty of murder?"

"In my experience, given the right circumstances, anyone can be tempted to murder."

"Well, I didn't know Miss Cummings, and though I don't like Millie, I don't hate her either. I'm not a murderer."

"What precipitated your fall on the runway?"

A lift of a pale shoulder was followed by, "I'm not sure."

"Did you find it slippery?"

"Not especially so. I felt a buzzing near my ear, and I swatted at it. Then I misstepped when I saw your girl, Miss Gold, go down. Nothing more sinister than that."

"A buzzing?" Ginger wondered if Alice had heard the sound of that third dart flying by.

"A rather large insect, by the sounds of it. It startled me. I had no intention of getting bitten. Then I fell."

"Who was with you last night?"

"Huh?"

Ginger nodded to the two glasses on the table. "Who helped you finish that bottle of vodka."

Miss White crossed her arms. "Not that it's any of your business, but I was with Bette Perry."

"The designer?" Ginger hadn't expected that answer.

"Unless there's more than one."

"I'm just a little surprised."

"Because designers don't usually spend their leisure time with models?"

Ginger shrugged. It *was* true.

"Well, Bette's not like that."

"You're on first-name terms?"

"It's amazing how close one can get when one

shares a bottle of vodka. We're good friends now." Miss White laughed. "You should see your face."

Ginger immediately erased her expression of shock. Keeping one's feelings and opinions to oneself was an important skill she mustn't go rusty on. "My face is fine, thank you, Miss White. Why were you and Miss Perry drinking together? Celebrating?"

"Hardly. Commiserating. Bette hadn't had a chance to show off her autumn line before all hell broke loose. She'd counted on the exposure and a good review by the reporters. She's relatively new as a designer, and it's very difficult to break the ranks. Now, if you don't mind, Mrs. Reed. I'm feeling rather under the weather."

14

Since she and Boss were in the area, Ginger impulsively pulled into the drive of St. George's Church. Though outside Hartigan House's South Kensington deanery, Ginger and her family had been attending St. George's since she and the vicar, the Reverend Oliver Hill, had become friends. The two had started a food service for street children called the Child Wellness Project, and her adopted son, Scout, had once benefited from the meals they provided.

An eighteenth-century construction, the church was built with sturdy limestone blocks and boasted a square castle-like turret and a bounty of beautiful stained glass. The nave had an attached hall and kitchen with the vicarage at the back.

Mrs. Davies, the stalwart church secretary with a perpetual smile, spotted Ginger from the hall and came outside to greet her. "Mrs. Reed, such a pleasant surprise!" She bent to pat Boss on the head. "And you're with your partner in crime."

Ginger laughed. "Hopefully, in crime-solving. Is the vicar or Mrs. Hill available? It's fine if they're busy. I came without an appointment."

"An appointment among friends is unnecessary, Mrs. Reed." She waved to the small stone house at the back of the property. "They're both at the vicarage."

"Tremendous," Ginger said. "I can make my way there."

"Very well," Mrs. Davies said. "Good day."

"Good day, Mrs. Davies."

The vicarage was a small edifice, the whole thing easily fitting into the drawing room of Hartigan House, but Matilda had done a fine job making it cosy and welcoming. The lady of the house broke into a surprised grin when she opened the door and saw Ginger and Boss standing there.

"Ginger!"

"I'm sorry for calling in unannounced."

Matilda waved Ginger inside. "It's not a problem

at all." She considered Ginger with a look of concern. "Is everything all right?"

"Oh yes, just a neighbourly visit, I promise. I've brought Boss with me."

"Welcome, Boss!" She turned to Ginger. "You're just in time for tea."

Ginger claimed an empty chair, the green-velvet upholstery showing signs of wear on the arms, and told Boss to lie at her feet.

Oliver stepped in, his red wavy hair barely tamed back with a goodly amount of oil, wearing his traditional look—a starchy white shirt and pressed black trousers.

"I thought I heard your voice," he said warmly.

"Hello, Oliver. I hope you don't mind my dropping in."

"Not at all, Ginger. You are like family to us now."

Matilda, who'd left them briefly, returned with a pink-cheeked baby in one arm.

"Little Margaret," Ginger said. "Look at her. Getting so big!"

"I'm already emotional at the thought of her growing up too fast," Oliver said. He took one of the empty chairs as Matilda handed the child over, propping his daughter on his lap.

"There's nothing that measures the speed of time like the way our children grow," Ginger agreed. "You're sure I'm not interrupting anything?"

"I was working on Sunday's sermon," Oliver said, "but was about to take a tea break."

Matilda rejoined them with a tea tray, and knowing everyone's preferences, added the milk and sugar and poured.

"Thank you," Ginger said, accepting hers. Boss put a paw on her leg, and Ginger patted his head. "You stay down."

"Now that my stomach's growing, it's just not comfortable to have him on my lap. Poor thing. I fear he's feeling rejected."

"Pets have a way of adapting," Matilda said. She put her tea down and reached for her daughter, giving Oliver a chance to sip his. She nodded to Ginger's girth. "How are you feeling these days?"

"Once in a while, I feel movement," Ginger told her. "It's like I've swallowed a butterfly."

As if he'd just remembered something dire, Oliver's countenance darkened suddenly. "We heard about the death at the fashion show," he said. "You must've suffered a shock."

"It was terribly shocking, that's true," Ginger said. But she'd had a lot of experience with death, not just with her job and Basil's, but her time spent in France during the war had, unfortunately, made her acquainted with loss of life.

"Thank you for providing an address for Miss White."

"Did you see her?" Matilda asked.

"Yes, which is why I'm in the area. I do believe she attends St. George's?"

"On occasion," Oliver replied.

"I realise there might be things you know in confidence," Ginger began, "but if there's anything you could tell me about her, I'd appreciate it."

"Is she a suspect?" Oliver asked.

"She and Millie Tatum got into a row before the show, and Millie was wounded in the affair. It's a matter of due diligence to follow up on a possible motive."

"I see," Oliver said. "Well, I hate to be unkind, but Miss White is—" He looked at Matilda for help.

"—rather spiteful." Matilda finished his sentence. "She seems to be more interested in the old testament story about an eye for an eye than Jesus' teachings about forgiving your enemies."

"Are you saying Miss White preferred to take her own revenge?"

"It sounds crass when you put it that way,"

Oliver said. "She did like to carry a grudge. Matilda once forgot to introduce her when a new gentleman entered their circle whilst mingling after church, and Miss White never fails to remind her of that oversight."

"Well," Matilda broke in, "he was a rather fetching bachelor."

Oliver laughed. "Who's married another since then."

Ginger sipped her tea. Miss White, the grudge-keeper, would remain firmly on her suspect list. Perhaps the model had worked with someone, and her fall off the stage had simply been a mode of diversion.

15

Ginger returned to Hartigan House—with only a few bruised kerbs and honking horns to guide her through the streets of London—in time for dinner. After parking in the garage, she strolled through the back floral-scented garden and the open French doors.

"The table is already set, madam," her maid Lizzie said. "Would you like me to take Boss and give him a bite to eat?"

Ginger handed the leash to Lizzie. "I'm sure he'd be delighted." Since moving to London from Boston, Boss had become a favourite of many people, Scout and Lizzie premium among them.

Thinking of Scout, she asked, "Would you happen to know where Scout is?"

"Last I saw him, madam, he was upstairs in the library working on his studies."

"Very good. Please let Mrs. Beasley know we'll be in the dining room in ten minutes. Is Mr. Reed here?"

Lizzie shook her head. "No, madam. I haven't seen him."

Since Basil's Austin wasn't in the garage, Ginger had surmised as much, but occasionally, he parked on the street in front of the house.

Upstairs, Ginger did, indeed, find Scout in the library, and to her surprise and great pleasure, found him with his little nose in a book.

"Hello, Scout."

"Oh, hello, Mum."

"I see you're enjoying an afternoon delving in literary pursuits?"

Scout crinkled his nose, then, when understanding dawned, smiled his crooked-tooth smile. "You mean reading!"

Ginger chuckled as she stepped into the room. After moving back to Hartigan House, she'd made it a point to refurbish the library and fill the shelves with volumes of both classic and modern fiction and non-fiction. When Scout moved in, she'd made sure there were plenty of titles to entice his curious mind, though this was the first she'd seen of him reading for himself rather than being read to. Though recently turning twelve, Scout had been late to begin his education and had only just mastered the alphabet. She flushed with pride.

"Billy Whiskers." His laughter bubbled as he held up the blue-bound book. "Such a funny goat!"

"Well, finish the page you're on, and then wash for dinner."

Scout slumped. "Yes, Mum."

Ginger slipped off her shoes in her room and dropped into one of the creamy-white pincushion armchairs that flanked both sides of the tall windows. The aqua-green wallpaper and white Persian carpets were a perfect backdrop to the ornate wooden furniture—a decorative four-poster bed she shared with Basil, a matching dressing table, and a chest of drawers. Inhaling deeply, she let the calm of the room fill her.

Removing her hat and gloves and placing them on the table beside her, Ginger resisted the urge to lie down, having missed her chance at that luxury for the day. Instead, she crossed the room to her dressing table and stared in the mirror. Her eyebrows constantly needed plucking, a painful exercise every fashionable lady carried out in the name of beauty, and she used her tweezers to catch a few strays from the thin, deeply arched brows. After that, she brushed her bob, then applied a jewelled hair comb to the left side of her head to hold the waves off her face. Her eyes landed on her bare ears—she couldn't believe she'd forgotten to clip on a pair of earrings that morning!

Ginger had many pairs to choose from, but she had the perfect set to match the yellow summer frock she wanted to wear. She fished through her jewellery box and frowned when she couldn't find them. She tried to remember the last time she'd worn them, and a memory of her lying in bed, having forgotten to remove them, came to mind. Right! She'd placed them in her bedside table drawer.

Even then, she had to dig through the collection of items tucked inside it. Somehow, one earring had ended up tucked underneath her old journal. Ginger took out the book and stroked it fondly. Inside the pages were memories of long ago, including fond ones of her late husband, Lord Daniel, and many about her trying, yet adventurous, times during the war. Thankfully, those dark days were over, and only bright ones shone ahead. She cupped her stomach, welcoming the new life growing there. Mourning may last for a night, but joy comes in the morning.

She placed the volume back in her bedside table drawer. After dressing and choosing a pair of shoes, Ginger clipped on her earrings and headed downstairs. She felt rather ravenous and eager to discover what scrumptious meal Mrs. Beasley had in store.

THE DINING ROOM, conveniently connected to the sitting room by a swinging door on one end, and a short corridor leading to the kitchen on the other, had, like the rest of the house, undergone a major renovation project when Ginger had moved back in. Before the modernisation, Hartigan House had been lost in the Victorian era's dark and cluttered style. Now the rooms were lighter, brighter, and simplified.

Ambrosia was already seated at her usual place at the long, glossy wooden table, just to the right of Ginger, who sat at one end. Basil, when he was present, claimed the other. It pleased Ginger to see that Felicia had found her way back from Feathers & Flair and that Scout had quickly joined her, washed, and was sitting immediately to her left.

"Good evening," Ginger said. "I hope you've all had a pleasant day."

"It was fine enough," Ambrosia grumbled.

"Once Millie left for home," Felicia said, "things

grew rather boring at the shop, so I saw no reason for me to stay there any longer. I spent a couple of hours at the investigative office working on my book instead."

Ginger noted that Felicia's usual sparkly good humour had yet to return and surmised that she hadn't heard from Charles. Or perhaps she had, and the news wasn't to her liking. She'd have to ask her about it once Scout and Ambrosia had left the table.

"Anything of interest happen while there?" Ginger asked.

Felicia shook her head. "Not to speak of."

Lizzie and Langley entered with trays of delicious-smelling dishes of roast beef and baked parsnips.

After a short word of thanks to the good Lord above, they greedily dug in.

Scout asked for gravy, then added, "When is Dad coming home?"

Ginger loved that Scout called Basil "Dad." There had been a day when he would have run and hidden from Basil simply because he was in law enforcement.

"I'm not sure," Ginger answered.

"He promised to take me to the tennis game tomorrow," Scout said.

"If for some reason he can't make it," Ginger replied, "I'll take you myself. In fact—" Thinking about Nellie Booth and how she'd like to interview the distraught athlete again, Ginger continued, "I'll come either way."

Unusually quiet, Ambrosia nibbled like a bird picking at a plum. On most days, she was ripe with opinionated pieces drawn from reading the newspapers or observing the family members' personal lives.

"Did the cat get your tongue, Grandmother?" Ginger asked her lightly.

Ambrosia settled her wide, heavy-lidded eyes on her. "What on earth does that mean?"

"You seem quieter than usual, that's all."

Ambrosia harrumphed. "Felicia, have you heard from Charles? When is he to return?"

Felicia frowned. "No, Grandmama. He's rather secretive when it comes to his life in France." Unexpectedly, Felicia burst into tears. "I fear he has a—" She glanced at Scout, who fortunately was busy sneaking bits of meat to Boss, who waited patiently at his feet. Felicia continued in a whisper. "An assignation. Some French hussy, I expect."

"Surely not!" Ambrosia sputtered.

Ginger couldn't venture an opinion. Many soldiers had appeased their loneliness by engaging

French women who took advantage of an opportunity to make money. Times had been hard, and Ginger didn't judge the women for doing what they thought they had to do to survive. It was quite likely that some real, long-lasting romances had developed during that time, and it was well documented that more than one British soldier had become a father to French children. Some maintained two families, one secret under the guise of business travels abroad.

Ginger smiled apologetically. "Felicia, love, I'm certain Charles has a perfectly honourable reason for travelling. A business venture, if I'm not mistaken."

Felicia pouted, "But why not ask me along?"

"Perhaps to preserve your reputation," Ambrosia said. "It's unseemly for a single lady to travel alone with a single gentleman, even if you should take Langley or Lizzie with you."

"May I leave the table, Mum?" Scout asked.

Ginger smirked. The conversation around the table by the Gold ladies must be mind-numbing for a child his age. Soon, though, the world of feminine intrigue would be all-consuming to him, and Ginger relished these short years yet left before young-manhood struck.

"You've finished eating?" she asked. His plate

was wiped clean, but he had been known to ask for seconds, occasionally.

"Yes, Mum."

"Very well. Take Boss with you."

Scout happily strolled away, calling Boss to join him at his heel.

Felicia, apparently ready to change the conversation, turned to Ginger. "Did you find Alice White?"

Ginger had mentioned her intention before leaving her shop. She'd found it prudent to let another know where she was going, especially during a murder investigation, if things went awry and she needed looking for. "I did. I'm afraid she wasn't very forthcoming."

With her mind back on the case, Ginger looked to Ambrosia. "Have you heard anything from your friend the Duchess of Worthington?"

Ambrosia snorted. "She's hardly my friend. Not even an acquaintance."

"She seems to think otherwise."

"She's confusing childhood nostalgia with friendship."

Ginger considered her grandmother-in-law. Though the Dowager Lady Gold liked to keep up appearances of social prestige, Ginger knew that the elderly lady had, in many ways, had a hard life. She'd lost her husband, then son and daughter-in-law, which made her the sole guardian of her grandchildren. And she'd almost lost Bray Manor, the family home in Chesterton. In fact, the Gold fortune had been in dire straits. If not for Ginger's marriage arrangement—she was then a Hartigan, from a wealthy Bostonian family—with Ambrosia's grandson Daniel, Ambrosia might've lost it all.

Ginger's curiosity about Ambrosia's hostility toward a childhood friend was piqued. "Normally, I wouldn't pry," Ginger said, "but the Duchess is related to the victim, Miss Cummings. Is there anything you can tell me about the Duchess that might help?"

Ambrosia raised a grey brow. "Cummings? Oh, that's right. I do recall that Deborah's sister Mary Ann Harvey—that was their maiden name—her daughter married a man by the name of Cummings."

"I find it highly coincidental that the Duchess' return to London after many years away would coincide with the purposeful death of her great-niece," Ginger said. "And that she just happened to be at the same event."

"I wouldn't trust Deborah as far as I could throw her," Ambrosia said, "but I'd hardly think she'd kill her great-niece. Whatever for? She has the world by the tail as it is. Besides, she wouldn't risk the notoriety should she be found out, much less the noose."

Ginger knew Ambrosia had failed to name the reason for her falling-out with her old friend. "I'm sure it's a long shot," she said, "but I must follow the evidence, no matter where it leads."

The swinging open of the dining-room door grabbed their attention.

"Hello, love," Ginger said as Basil stepped into the room. "So good that you could join us, if a tad late."

"Hello, ladies." Basil took his seat at the opposite end of the table.

Ginger rang for Lizzie, and the maid arranged for hot food to be brought.

"So, what did I miss?" Basil asked.

Ginger decided to hold off sharing the details of her morning enquiries until she and Basil were alone. She expected Basil would do the same for her.

"Not much, love," she said. "Any news on your end that you can share?"

"Only that the inquest date has been set for two days from now. You and Felicia shall be called to testify, of course."

"Oh blast!" Felicia said. "I do detest inquests."

"I find them rather interesting," Ginger said.

Felicia sniffed. "I find them morbid."

Ginger smiled at her disgruntled sister-in-law. "At any rate, we must both oblige the law," she said. And she hoped the event would shed light on who had murdered Irene Cummings and why.

16

On Monday, the tennis matches were in full swing when Ginger, Basil, and Scout arrived at the tennis club. Finding seats near the front, Ginger was glad she'd remembered to bring her parasol, for the sun was high and hot. Even with her shaded spot, she felt herself on the verge of perspiring. As it was, her growing child within made Ginger more susceptible to warmth, and she had to use a handkerchief to mop her brow.

"Are you all right, love?" Basil asked.

"I'm fine," Ginger said. "I seem less able to tolerate the heat than when I was younger."

Ginger was only thirty-three, not nearly approaching midlife. And many women gave birth in their thirties—but not for the first time. In that respect, Ginger was an anomaly. Having conceived at this point in her life was a surprise as Ginger had attempted a family with her first husband to no avail. No effort had been made with Basil to prevent one, yet many months had passed since their wedding night.

The baby was a blessing—just as Ginger had been to her parents. However, her mother, also having conceived late in life, had died shortly after Ginger was born. Ginger shuddered at the thought. Would she be strong enough to survive this birth? Matilda had reassured her that medicine had come a long way since 1893.

A men's singles game was in play. Scout pointed. "Douglas Boyd and Robert Armstrong."

Both men were fit and energetic and looked dapper in their tennis outfits of white cotton trousers and white short-sleeved shirts.

The match ended three sets to love, with Douglas Boyd winning. Robert Armstrong threw his racquet onto the ground near his coach's feet, and Ginger frowned at the display of poor sportsmanship.

A women's singles match came next, and Ginger squinted as the athletes came onto the court, dressed in what looked like Patou sportswear with long pleated skirts and matching long-sleeved white blouses. The dark-haired player looked familiar.

"Is that Nellie Booth?" she asked.

Basil stared at the woman. "It appears so."

"She's not leaving herself much time to mourn," Ginger said. "Perhaps she shed all of her tears last night."

"It's an important game, Mum," Scout said. "The winner moves up the ranking. Perhaps even plays at Wimbledon next year."

"Is that so? Was Miss Cummings supposed to play?"

Scout shrugged and slipped into his lazy street dialect. "Dunno."

Basil checked the programme they had been given when they arrived. "It appears that Miss Booth was meant to play against Miss Cummings. Someone had the task of scratching her name out of all the programmes and adding a substitute."

"Who would that be?" Ginger asked.

"A Miss Ryerson."

"She's not as good as Miss Cummings," Scout said.

Ginger gazed at her son. "How do you know?"

"I've seen her play, and she's got a lower overall ranking."

Basil read the back of the programme. "The rankings are listed here. Scout's right."

"So," Ginger mused, "with Miss Cummings out, Miss Booth has a better chance of climbing to the top."

"Indeed," Basil said, "but highly circumstantial."

"I wonder if Mr. Armstrong cried all his tears out last night too," Scout said.

Ginger's attention snapped to her son. "What do you mean?"

"Mr. Armstrong was sweet on Miss Cummings. I heard a couple of ladies talk about it." He curled a lip. "Waste of time, if you ask me. Who cares about romance?"

Ginger's attention moved between Miss Booth and Miss Ryerson, Miss Booth clearly with the upper hand, and a moody Robert Armstrong watching from the sidelines.

"I'm going to stretch my legs," Ginger said. The discomfort of the hard chairs had convinced her to stand. "I won't be gone long."

Basil, ever the gentleman, helped her to her feet. "I'd like to hear what he has to say as well," he whispered,

Oh, how well her husband knew her!

Ginger meandered around the circumference of

the court until she reached the area where Mr. Armstrong sat. "Exciting game, isn't it?" she said casually.

Mr. Armstrong did a double take when he turned to her. Ginger was used to receiving the admiration of the opposite sex and offered a dazzling smile, pushed a lock of her red bob behind one ear, and blinked her eyelashes. Once again, she was glad that the fashion of the day did wonders for hiding a growing stomach, though Ginger had started holding her handbag in front of her as extra concealment.

Her friendly nature was rewarded, and Mr. Armstrong, running a hand over his glossy hair, flashed a smile in return. "In a word," he said.

"So sad about Miss Cummings," Ginger remarked. "I understand she was meant to play this game with Miss Booth."

"And a far more exciting game it would've been. Such a terrible loss for the tennis world."

Not exactly the reaction of a broken-hearted boyfriend.

"Aren't you Robert Armstrong?" Ginger gushed. "I've seen your photograph in the newspaper!"

Mr. Armstrong smiled crookedly as if he were doing his best to look self-effacing. "Yes, that's me."

Pressing a finger of her gloved hand to her lips,

Ginger spoke conspiratorially, "Weren't you and Miss Cummings courting?"

"Well, at one time. But it had gone cold. Still, I didn't wish her any harm. And if I find out who hurt her . . ." He pushed his palm with a fist. ". . . He'll be sorry!"

Ginger hummed and turned her eyes back to the game in time to see Nellie Booth nail an overarm shot and score. The crowd applauded politely.

Mr. Armstrong cleared his throat. "I didn't catch your name, miss?"

Ginger smiled and extended her gloved hand. "Mrs. Reed. It's a pleasure to meet you."

As expected, Mr. Armstrong's eyes flashed briefly with disappointment, but he recovered quickly. "Do enjoy the rest of the game, Mrs. Reed."

"I will. Thank you."

Ginger wandered back to her seat between Basil and Scout.

"How was your walkabout, love?" Basil asked, his green-brown eyes staring at her pointedly.

Ginger hadn't yet revealed that she was working for Miss Chanel and would wait until they had a private moment later that night to do so. But Basil was also working on the case, and it behoved her to share her findings.

"Mr. Armstrong admitted to a relationship with Miss Cummings but said it had grown cold."

"Is that so?" Basil said.

"Unfortunately, we can't get Miss Cummings' perspective. What if she wanted more? Perhaps marriage? Did she have leverage that could ruin Mr. Armstrong's career?"

"If so," Basil said, "that would be motive. I'll have my men investigate Mr. Armstrong's background and financial history."

As GINGER GUESSED, and a myriad of sports gamblers had probably bet, Nellie Booth won her game. She effortlessly sprang across the court like a gazelle in a meadow, her toothy smile bright in the afternoon sun. To Ginger's surprise, Nellie Booth headed directly for Robert Armstrong, who gave her a friendly handshake. Miss Booth beamed up at him with a look that said she'd like to be more than friendly.

If they weren't already.

Unlike Mr. Armstrong, Miss Ryerson took her loss with grace, and after shaking hands with Miss Booth, had returned to her coach with her chin held high.

"Is that it?" Ginger asked.

Basil referred to the programme, but Scout answered. "It's the last game today. Might I come again tomorrow?"

Ginger glanced at Basil. She knew that he was taking time off work and that Superintendent Morris would frown deeply should it happen again tomorrow. She felt rather wilted from the heat and didn't relish repeating the sequence tomorrow.

"Perhaps," she said, "if Mr. Fuller is willing to escort you. Your father and I have work to do."

The offer seemed to appease Scout as it was likely his tutor would be up to the task.

Ginger had just taken Basil's arm as he assisted her from her seat when a shriek cut through the normal chatter, followed by a corporate gasp and sharp questioning.

Miss Booth was on the ground.

Had she fainted? Or worse.

"I have to run over there," Basil said. Ginger nodded, watching him go. She took Scout's hand. "We must follow."

"What happened to her, Mum?"

"I don't know. Perhaps the heat was too much, and she simply fainted." Ginger hoped that was the case, but her instinct told her it was something more nefarious.

"Excuse me," she said when she reached the crowd now huddled around Nellie Booth's prone form. "I'm with the police."

That wasn't technically true, but she *was* with Basil, a chief inspector. When she made it to the inner circle, she groaned. Nellie Booth's lips were blue.

A nurse had her fingers to Miss Booth's neck. She wrinkled her nose. "I think there's a pulse."

A doctor pushed through, his stethoscope at the ready. "She's alive, but her pulse is very weak. She must be hospitalised immediately."

Before long, an ambulance arrived, and a stretcher was carried towards Miss Booth's body. Ginger noticed Mr. Armstrong watching from a distance, looking if Ginger had to call it, rather bored. Two female tennis players, romantically attached to Mr. Armstrong, had been brought down—one was dead, one nearly dead.

Ginger scowled in the man's direction. She didn't believe in coincidence *that* much.

Basil drew closer. "Perhaps you should accompany Scout home?"

Ginger agreed that removing Scout from a

disturbing incident involving someone he admired was the responsible thing to do. She took Scout by the hand and hired a taxicab to drive them back to Hartigan House.

"Is she going to be all right, Mummy?"

Ginger gazed at her son with compassion. When she and Scout were first acquainted, and later when he'd become her ward, he'd called her "Missus". Once she'd decided that her heart demanded more from the child and had decided to adopt, she asked that he call her "Mum", which, over time, he'd learned to do.

But "Mummy" was a handle he used only in times of uncertainty or duress. She tightly squeezed his hand.

"I do hope so. Rest assured, she's in the best possible hands. Dad will do his best to find out what happened."

The ride in the black taxicab was uneventful, and soon, they were parked in front of Hartigan House. A black wrought-iron fence divided the front garden from the two-storey limestone house. Tall windows graced each floor, and numerous chimneys dotted the roof of the gable attic that housed the live-in staff. Ginger paid the driver, and she and Scout headed up the stone path to the front door.

Pippins was already there to greet them. Ginger was amazed by how her butler managed to be there when needed—as if he had a sixth sense as to when she, or anyone really, was to arrive.

"Madam," he said, his cornflower-blue eyes twinkling. They always did when he watched Ginger, his fondness for his mistress going back to when she was a babe in a bassinet.

"Dear Pippins," Ginger said. "I'm afraid young Scout had a bit of a shock. One of the tennis players, Nellie Booth, was taken away by ambulance."

"I do hope Miss Booth will be all right."

"As do we. Would you mind taking Scout to the kitchen for some refreshment? I'm sure one of Mrs. Beasley's biscuits and a glass of milk would do the trick."

Scout's worried frown reversed into a grin of anticipation. "It's fine, Pippins," he said. "I know my way to the kitchen."

As Scout scampered away, Pippins observed, "The young master is growing up."

Ginger agreed. "Too quickly. Once the baby arrives, he'll seem gigantic, I'm sure."

"Would you like me to arrange for tea, madam?" Pippins asked.

"That would be lovely. Please have Lizzie bring it to my bedroom."

Ginger gripped the railing of the curved staircase—the only barrier between herself and a good rest—and heaved herself up the stairs.

17

The inquest was held the next morning at the Old Bailey courthouse. Ginger decided on a simple grey dress with a matching summer jacket, feeling it was appropriate for the solemn occasion. She had been summoned because she'd been the hostess at the event, and Basil was called as he was the first police officer of note on the scene. Across the room, Ginger made eye contact with the designers: Kate Reily, Jean Patou, Coco Chanel, and Elsa Schiaparelli. Their assistants, including Jean-Luc Marchand, sat in a row behind them.

The rest of the seats were taken by other members of the police, as well as curious onlookers. The Duchess of Worthington was among them.

The coroner, a willowy, hunched-over man, entered the room and took his seat behind the desk at the front of the room. "Might I have your attention," he said. "This inquest is regarding the untimely death of one Miss Irene Cummings. This is not a trial but a means to establish the identity of the deceased, and the circumstances of her death."

Not merely an onlooker, the Duchess of Worthington was the first to be summoned. *Of course*, Ginger thought, *a family member to identify the deceased.*

The Duchess approached the stand in such a regal manner, one would be forgiven if one thought that Queen Mary herself had been called to the stand. Lifting the mid-length skirt of her stylish frock, she accepted the assistance of a court attendant with the other. Her white gloves reached elbows that appeared to be made of papier mâché.

Once the Duchess was positioned to give evidence, the coroner said, "Please state your name for the records."

"Deborah, Duchess of Worthington."

"And your relationship to the deceased?"

"She was my great-niece. My sister's daughter's daughter."

Her Grace didn't show any emotion, which

Ginger thought was preferable to a demonstration of grief that was insincere.

"And can you confirm that the deceased at the mortuary is, in fact, Miss Irene Cummings?"

"I can."

The coroner lowered his chin. "Thank you, Your Grace. You may return to your seat." After reviewing his notes, he said, "I call Mrs. Basil Reed to the stand."

Ginger walked gracefully across the floor to the witness stand, resisting the urge to cup her growing belly with her palm—a new habit sure to highlight the nature of her condition, and something she most definitely didn't want to do.

She took her seat, and the coroner began.

"Mrs. Reed, it's my understanding that you helped to organise the fashion show held in Hyde Park?"

"That's correct."

"Please give a brief outline of the timeline of events, as you remember them."

"Yes," Ginger, sitting straight with gloved hands cupped on her lap, began, "I arranged for a crew to set up the runway and designer tents very early in the morning. And I hired the models. Most of the designers arrived with their assistants around eight a.m." Ginger caught Coco's eyes. "Only Mademoiselle Chanel failed to be present at that time."

The coroner furrowed his brow as he read his notes. "Can you confirm that there was a model substitution?"

"Yes. Miss Felicia Gold was brought in as a last-minute replacement."

"And she is a professional model as well?"

"No, sir. But she's familiar with the industry."

"I see. And when did the incident in question occur?"

"About forty-five minutes into the show."

"Had you met the deceased before that time."

"No, I had not; I knew her by reputation."

"And that was?"

"A fine tennis player rapidly going up the rankings."

"Then she wasn't a model by profession either?"

"No. Not all the models were."

"And why was Miss Cummings modelling on this occasion?"

Ginger's eyes darted to Jean Patou.

"It was at the request of Monsieur Patou. He thought it would be good promotion for his new sports line to have a prominent athlete display his outfits."

Satisfied, the coroner said, "Thank you, Mrs. Reed."

Ginger rose from her seat as the coroner referred to his notes.

"Would Monsieur Patou please come to the stand?"

Monsieur Patou, debonair in his cotton suit with cuffed trousers and bow tie, stood behind the witness box.

The coroner began, "What was your relationship to the deceased?"

"We had no relationship," Monsieur Patou replied with his prominent French accent. "She was a simple girl I hired for this one occasion."

"And how did you end up choosing her for your demonstration?" the coroner asked.

"I asked my circle of acquaintances who might be an appropriate choice. Height, weight, overall look, that sort of thing."

"And who recommended Miss Cummings?"

Monsieur Patou paused. "I believe it was Mademoiselle Chanel's assistant."

A soft murmur erupted at this revelation.

The coroner used his gavel to draw the group to order. "Might I remind you that no one is on trial here today? Now, if we may proceed, I shall call Chief Inspector Basil Reed to give evidence."

Basil scooted past Ginger, walked across the room, and replaced Monsieur Patou at the stand.

"We'll be brief," the coroner said to him. "Is it true that you were the first police officer on the scene?"

"Yes."

"And were you able to determine how the deceased came by her death?"

"Only that a dart had been shot from somewhere near the back of the stage and said dart had punctured the victim's neck. The object was found in the grass later."

After Basil, the medical examiner, Dr. Wood, was called to the stand.

"Dr. Wood, are you able to elaborate on the preceding evidence? Do you know how the deceased came by her death, and can you determine the time of death?"

"Since there were witnesses in the tent at the time she succumbed, the time of death is close to three thirty p.m. As for the cause, I am assuming it was due to a poison having been applied to the tip of the dart. However, I've yet to determine the nature of the poison in question. None of the usual culprits apply."

Dr. Wood was excused, and Felicia was called.

After a few identifying questions, Felicia answered the more pertinent one. "No, I have no reason to believe I was targeted. In fact, I'm embarrassed to admit, I simply tripped over my own two feet."

When the rest of the designers and models offered no new evidence, the coroner called the inquest to a close.

"I believe we have been presented with enough evidence," the coroner stated. "My verdict is wilful murder by a person or persons unknown."

It was the expected pronouncement, and though a low murmuring bubbled in the room, no one expressed surprise or dissent.

Ginger's eye was drawn to the Duchess. Laying a palm on Basil's arm, she said, "Excuse me, love. I'm going to see if I can catch the Duchess before she leaves."

"And I would like a word with Mr. Armstrong," Basil returned. "Let's meet at the front door."

Ginger, finding it rather challenging to walk quickly with her extra weight and shoes that inexplicably felt too tight, reached the slower-moving Duchess, impeded slightly by her entourage.

"Your Grace!" Ginger called.

The Duchess stopped and turned to Ginger's voice.

"Might I have a moment of your time?"

Glancing about the room, the Duchess' gaze settled on Ginger. "Mrs. Reed?"

"I'd like to ask a few questions about Irene, if you wouldn't mind?"

The Duchess sniffed. "I fear we won't have much privacy here. Why don't you come to the house for tea?"

"I'd be delighted," Ginger said, and they settled on a time.

"Very good." The Duchess' expression remained neutral. "Please do invite Ambrosia. It's been a frightfully long time since we chatted, and I'm starting to get the feeling she's trying to avoid me."

"I'm sure she's not," Ginger said generously, knowing the chances of Ambrosia agreeing to have tea with the Duchess were slim. "I'll let her know you've asked about her."

As the Duchess left the room, Coco Chanel stepped into view. "Such nonsense bringing up poor Jean-Luc like that," she mewed to Ginger. "As if being informed about who's who in a national sport is a crime. These inquests . . ." Coco flicked a gloved hand. "Such a waste of time, no? I could have told you Miss Cummings was murdered by person or persons unknown."

"It's a legal process to establish the fact officially," Ginger said.

"Well, have you learned anything new? Am I still a suspect?"

"I'm afraid so," Ginger said. "But the investigation is ongoing. I'll let you know as soon as I find something useful."

"Do make it snappy. I am due to return to Paris shortly. I have another event there, and it would make everyone immensely unhappy if I were to miss it."

Ginger forced a smile. "Of course. Ta-ta for now."

Coco wiggled the fingers of her gloved hand. "*Au revoir.*"

18

Amused by Ginger's tea date with the Duchess of Worthington, Basil didn't believe that the older lady would have anything new to contribute to solving the case. She had been in the audience at the time of her great-niece's death and surrounded by her people. Even if she'd had the opportunity to slip away, Basil could hardly envision the lady having the vascular capacity to launch a dart, not to mention the skill to hit the mark.

He was about to head back to Scotland Yard to collect Braxton, but something about the way Robert Armstrong ducked out of the inquest bothered him. Basil was certain that the tennis player had seen him lift a hand, indicating he'd like a word, but instead, the man had hurried out like a shot.

Basil had a list of addresses for potential suspects in his suit pocket. Upon reviewing the folded piece of paper, he confirmed Mr. Armstrong's residence in White City. There was no way to know if Mr. Armstrong had headed directly home, but there was only one way to find out.

At a former red-brick warehouse converted into flats, Basil knocked on the door he presumed belonged to Mr. Armstrong, but if the man was in, he wasn't answering. Basil tested the knob but found the door locked. No sounds came from the other side, no footsteps, nor radio, nor running of the tap, nor blowing of the kettle whistle.

Disappointed, Basil lumbered down the steps. He immediately saw a door with a sign saying "Proprietress" on it. He knocked, and a woman with greying hair and wrinkling skin opened the door.

When she saw him, she frowned. Hoping to disarm her, he removed his hat.

"Forgive my intrusion. I'm looking for a friend of mine, Robert Armstrong, but I fear I've missed him. Would you happen to know how he spends his afternoons? When he's not playing tennis, that is."

"Check the Hart and Quail pub around the corner. The fellows in this building practically live there, and they're loud about letting me know when they come back. I don't care much, so long as they pay up on time, you know what I'm saying?"

Basil thanked the manageress and walked around the corner. The narrow brick building that housed the Hart and Quail was blood red with matching red window shutters. Low ceilings were suited for a generation of short-statured men, and Basil had to remove his hat and duck his head. Squinting into the dimly lit room, Basil had to wait momentarily for his eyes to adjust as he scoured the heads. Seated alone at a corner table with only a tall glass for company, sat Robert Armstrong—his athletic physique hard to miss.

Basil claimed an empty chair for himself at Armstrong's table. Startled, Armstrong jerked his head up. The man's eyes were rimmed red, and his cheeks were flushed from too much drink or emotion resulting from the inquest, Basil didn't know which.

"Oh," Armstrong muttered.

"Mind if I join you?" Basil said. He set his hat on a seat beside him and smoothed out the lapels of his summer suit.

The man mumbled into his drink, "I doubt I have much choice, do I?"

"I understand you and Miss Cumming were a couple," Basil said.

"'Were' is right. We weren't anymore when—" He gulped. "I know we had broken up, but she was once my sweetheart, and I didn't wish her any harm."

Basil trained his gaze on the man. Too often, when a woman was murdered, the person closest to her in her life was to blame for her demise.

"Who broke things off?"

Armstrong sighed mournfully. "I did, I suppose."

"Either you did, or you didn't."

"Okay. It was me. I ended things."

"How did Miss Cummings take that?" Basil asked.

"Not well. She had a bloody fit, shouting so loudly that the people in the flat next door complained to the manager."

"Did she threaten you?"

Armstrong's eyes shot up. "Who told you that?"

It was a guess on Basil's part. "What did she say?"

"Just rot like she'd see me hung by my manly parts, if you know what I mean. Irene was very competitive, on the court and off, and foul-mouthed, for a lady."

"Who was she competing with when it came to you, Mr. Armstrong?"

"See here, I didn't mean—"

"Miss Booth?"

Armstrong seemed like he was having trouble keeping up, and Basil wondered how many glasses the man had emptied.

"D-did she tell you that?" he blustered.

"Is it true?"

"Yes, but only once, and believe me, it was a mistake."

Basil had seen how Miss Booth had acted in Armstrong's presence at the game. "Does she know that?"

He shrugged. "Well, I know what it looks like."

"It looks like you had two ladies who were inconveniencing your life and possibly interfering with your concentration during your games—I saw you lose, Mr. Armstrong—and I wonder how tempting it would have been for you to be rid of them both."

"That's bloody rubbish! And you've got no proof. I wasn't anywhere near Irene when she died nor Nellie when she fell."

"That's the problem right there," Basil said. "You don't have a solid alibi for either event. You could've shot the dart at Miss Cummings and found a way to poison Miss Booth."

Armstrong snorted. "Well, if I did, you have your work cut out proving it, haven't you?"

19

*A*mbrosia told Ginger, in no uncertain terms, she would not, under any circumstances, have tea with Deborah Harvey. When Ginger pressed her for reasons, she muttered something under her breath that sounded like "betrayal of the sisterhood" and stomped away, her walking stick smacking the marble-tiled floor as she went.

The Worthingtons' townhouse in Mayfair was not far from where Basil had once lived. Ginger approached the front door and made use of the iron knocker. A butler opened the door and dutifully stared down his nose at her.

"Good afternoon. I'm Mrs. Reed. The Duchess of Worthington is expecting me."

"Yes, Her Grace did inform me. She will receive you in her sitting room, madam."

Ginger followed the butler down a broad and bright corridor, beyond a set of white doors, and into a delightful sitting room. The Duchess, sitting poker-straight on a padded high-backed, green-velvet chair, gracefully motioned to the matching chair sitting empty. "Welcome, Mrs. Reed. Please have a seat."

Ginger did as bid. "Thank you, Your Grace."

"I see Ambrosia didn't come along."

"I'm afraid she had a previous engagement."

The Duchess appeared sincerely disappointed. "Of course she did."

Ginger removed her gloves and slipped them into her handbag. "I hope you don't mind me saying so, but I can't help but sense that there is bad blood between the two of you."

The Duchess' lips twitched. "You're the detective."

A maid entered with a tray with a tea set and a plate of small triangular salmon and cucumber sandwiches and placed it on the tea table between the ladies before wordlessly leaving them alone.

As the Duchess poured for them, Ginger waited to see if she would elaborate on what had soured her friendship with Ambrosia, but instead, she nodded in polite acknowledgment to the bump Ginger could no longer hide, at least not whilst sitting.

"You're in the family way, I see. Congratulations."

"Thank you, this is my first. Basil and I also have an adopted son."

"How quaint."

"Do you have children?"

The Duchess' hand shook as she lowered her cup onto its saucer. "No. The Duke and I weren't blessed in that way."

Ginger had the distinct feeling there was more to that story, more sorrow, than Her Grace was letting on.

Changing the subject, the Duchess said, "That was the first inquest I've ever been to. I imagine, in your line of work, you've been to a few."

Ginger sipped her tea. "I have."

"I still can't believe Irene is gone."

"How is her family?"

"Shattered."

"Did her parents or siblings ever come to London to watch her play tennis?"

"On occasion. Irene plays, er, played a lot, so it wasn't possible for them to see every game. They're waiting for her body to be released and transported to Chesterton so that they can give her a proper burial. I don't suppose you know how long that will take?"

"The pathologist has to complete the post-mortem first," Ginger said. "I'm certain he's working tirelessly to determine the cause of death."

"You mean the type of poison used?"

"Yes."

"Such a strange way to come to one's end," the Duchess said. "Rather exotic." As if she approved of "exotic" modes of dying, her lips twitched again.

Ginger couldn't help but wonder if the Duchess was, in fact, guilty of the crime, though she would've had to engage an accomplice. Not such a far-fetched idea. She had recently left Morocco where one might obtain a rare poison and had just happened to be in London at the time of the show where her great-niece was modelling. Though she claimed not to have spoken to Miss Cummings beforehand, they only had the Duchess' word on that. She could be lying about not knowing that her great-niece would be in the fashion show until the day of the event.

The question in that scenario would be why? What could be the Duchess' motive?

"I must confess, I'm surprised that you've not

gone back to Chesterton to be with your family during this difficult time," Ginger said.

The Duchess tilted her head. "Is that so? Your own husband has forbidden me to leave London. And I think I was quite clear about the fact that my sister and I are estranged."

"Of course," Ginger admitted. "I only thought, that under the circumstances, you might've reached out, perhaps with a telegram or telephone call?"

"You're quite interested in my personal affairs, Mrs. Reed." The Duchess' lips twitched again. "But I'll humour you for Irene's sake. As I've implied, my sister and I aren't close. We grew distant after my wedding. My marriage wasn't exactly celebrated, you see." She glanced at her age-spotted hands wistfully. "Fifty-five years is a terribly long time to wait to mend bridges. Rather too long, it would seem."

As she sipped her tea, Ginger wondered how impertinent it would be to ask why the Duchess' marriage wasn't celebrated, but it could hardly have anything to do with the death of Miss Cummings, and so she bit her tongue.

However, it would be impolite not to enquire about the Duke of Worthington at all. "How is His Grace?" she asked. "Shall he be joining you in London soon?"

"Theodore is a military man—fought in both Boer Wars and the Great War— and I doubt we'll see him here until the Rif war is over. The fighting in Morocco is fierce and Theo's not a young man anymore, so can hardly engage in actual battles. He's in Spain at the moment, hobnobbing with the generals."

"I do hope he is keeping out of danger."

"Yes, one can hope," the Duchess said, but Ginger got the distinct impression that Her Grace didn't care too terribly about her husband's welfare, displaying little evidence of missing his company.

The rest of Ginger's time with the Duchess was frustratingly uneventful. The Duchess was adept at keeping the conversation benign with tiresome tributes to the pleasant summer weather London was experiencing or occasional comments revealing her less-than-joyous time spent in Spain. The entire visit had lasted not even an hour before the Duchess declared the need for an afternoon rest, something that Ginger, at that moment, envied.

However, she pushed the growing fatigue she felt to the side and drove to the University College Hospital, where she found Nellie Booth, with five others, resting in a bright, white-washed ward, under white sheets and blankets. The bed frames, made of metal piping, were also painted white, and the space had a distinct antiseptic feel about it. The patient next to Nellie slept soundly, the quiet interrupted by intermittent blasts of snorts and snoring.

On seeing Ginger enter the ward, Nellie shifted herself into a seated position, adjusting her pillows until she found comfort. Ginger thought the girl, despite her ordeal, looked particularly well.

"Good afternoon, Miss Booth. I hope I'm not intruding on your rest," Ginger said softly,

"Not at all. Quite honestly, I'm getting rather bored. Like I told the doctors, I feel fine, but they want to keep me an extra day for observation. I was hoping for a visitor!"

Nellie's enthusiasm was returned by a bout of snorting from her unconscious hospital neighbour.

Nellie and Ginger shared a smile, sharing a sense of borrowed embarrassment for the woman.

"Is she all right?" Ginger whispered.

"Sedated," Nellie said. "I don't know what's the matter with her. At least if she's snoring, I know she's not dead. I couldn't deal with another death; I just couldn't!"

Ginger sat in the empty wooden visitor's chair. "Do the doctors know yet, what happened to you?"

Nellie wrinkled her nose. "Not yet, but they

don't think I was naturally overheated, and neither do I. I'm an athlete. I play hard all the time, and in sunnier and warmer conditions."

"What do you think caused it?"

Nellie leaned in and lowered her voice as if she was afraid her snoring companion might hear despite her deep sleep. "I think someone is trying to kill me, Mrs. Reed. Just like they killed Irene. I don't really feel that safe here."

"I saw a constable in the hallway," Ginger said. "I'm sure you're perfectly fine."

"I hope so."

"Why would someone want to kill you?"

"I don't know. Why would they kill Irene? I can only guess that someone is jealous of how well we were doing with our tennis."

Ginger pushed a lock of her red bob behind her ear. "It's my understanding that Miss Cummings ranked higher than you and that her demise has improved your standing."

"I suppose that's true but purely serendipitous. I'd much rather earn my way up than have it handed to me. I'm just lucky I wasn't permanently injured by my attacker, and I can keep playing." Her eyes brightened. "I have a big game coming up. If I win, I'll get to play against Suzanne Lenglen!"

"Tell me about Robert Armstrong."

Nellie's smile fell. "What about him?"

"He and Irene were close, weren't they?"

"Yes, for a while."

"And I heard that, perhaps, the two of you are close now?"

Nellie shrugged. "Not really. We're both too busy with tennis to commit to anything serious."

Ginger conceded that might be true, but there was likely quite a lot of time for non-committed liaisons.

Nellie filled in the silence by adding, "Bobbie had had enough of Irene. She was clingy and wanted marriage. I didn't understand it myself, since matrimony would've killed her career, but she just didn't care about tennis as much as I do."

"And yet she ranked higher than you?"

"Sheer luck!" Nellie was rankled, but she reined in her emotions. She smoothed out her bedsheets and rearranged her face. "Irene happened to play well when it counted. I, unfortunately, have had a few off days. But that didn't make her the better player."

Ginger thought the Lawn Tennis Association would disagree but kept that thought to herself.

Nellie continued, "Bobbie and Irene weren't

meant to last. He told me himself he'd do anything to get rid of Irene." She raised a dark brow. "Not to speak ill of the dead, but Irene was like a leech when it came to poor Bobbie. Now, if you don't mind, Mrs. Reed, I'm frightfully exhausted."

"Of course." Ginger secured her handbag and got to her feet. "I wish you a speedy recovery, and hopefully, we'll soon learn the reason behind your collapse."

"Thank you," Nellie muttered, adding a yawn for good measure.

Her hospital mate snorted loudly, arousing herself. "Oh, hello," she said, looking sheepish. "I hope I didn't miss tea."

20

Ginger had one last stop to make before returning to Hartigan House, where she desperately wanted to retreat to her bedroom and nap! But Ginger realised she hadn't followed up her interview with Alice White nor with her questions, particularly those concerning designer Bette Perry.

Finding a red phone box, Ginger parked at the kerb—well, slightly on the kerb—and stepped inside. A phone book hung on a chain and, after removing a glove, Ginger flipped through the pages with her long, manicured nails until she reached the *P* section. Running her fingernail down the surnames, she paused at "E. Perry." Elizabeth? It was the only E. Perry in the book, and though the majority of

London residents didn't have a personal telephone, those who had ambitions to excel in business often did. Bette Perry was a competitive business lady, and Ginger wouldn't be surprised if she answered the number assigned to E. Perry.

Ginger lifted the receiver then waited for the operator to connect the call.

A lady with a soft voice answered, "Perry Designs."

"Hello, this is Mrs. Reed of Lady Gold Investigations. I'm hoping to speak to Miss Bette Perry."

"Speaking. How can I help you, Mrs. Reed?"

"Oh, hello, Miss Perry. I'm making enquiries about the death of Miss Irene Cummings and hope to speak to each designer who was at the show. Would you be willing to spare a few moments of your time to speak to me?"

"I don't see why not. When?"

Ginger checked her wristwatch. "I could be at your studio in fifteen minutes."

"So soon? I'm rather busy, but all right."

When Miss Perry opened the door to her flat, she didn't nod to the empty chair nor make any gesture of welcome. "I have a large order to fulfil, so I don't have time to dilly-dally. I'm afraid we'll have to make this quick."

"Very well," Ginger said. "I'll get right to the point. I understand that you and Miss Alice White are acquainted."

"Yes, what of it?"

"I've been in the fashion industry for a long time, Miss Perry, and I know it's rather unusual for designers and models to socialise in a non-professional setting."

"What are you getting at?"

"I called in to see Miss White and found the remnants of a party for two."

Miss Perry shrugged. "I suppose I like to break the mould. I'm not much into this class nonsense. It's all a façade, anyway. Do you know that Coco Chanel is a rags-to-riches story? Apparently, she works hard to conceal her origins of poverty, but I've been told she was abandoned by her father and raised by nuns."

"I suppose we all have a right to our secrets," Ginger said coolly. "I only ask about your little soirée with Miss White as part of my enquiries regarding the death of Miss Cummings."

"I'm afraid I don't see what my sharing a drink with a friend has to do with that."

"It was more than one drink and shared on a night of tragedy in the industry. It leads me to believe there was more to it. Perhaps you or Miss White know something about the affair that might help the police with the case?"

"Then why aren't the police standing on my step? Answer me that." Miss Perry had the propensity for rudeness but was intelligent enough to keep herself from burning bridges. Otherwise, Ginger wouldn't have been surprised to have the door shut in her face.

"Now, as I said, I'm busy."

Ginger knew a dead end when she saw it. "Thank you for your time, Miss Perry."

Back in the Crossley, Ginger rested her head as fatigue threatened. All she wanted was her bed and little Boss at her side for comfort and thought it an excellent idea to head back to Hartigan House.

Upon arriving, Ginger headed up the staircase, but as she reached the landing, she heard what could only be described as "a rumpus" coming from Felicia's bedroom.

Poking her head through the cracked-open door, Ginger gaped. Though not one for strict tidiness, Felicia did have certain standards she was currently upsetting. The doors of her wooden wardrobe were wide open, and its contents were spewed across the room as if a whirlwind had exploded from inside. Felicia sat on the pink-padded bench at the foot of her bed, trying on one shoe at a time, and when the item failed to pass muster, she threw it like a designer missile at the hardwood floor.

"Felicia?"

Her face pinched with emotion, Felicia turned towards Ginger to reveal tears passing through heavy mascara, causing charcoal lines to run down her cheeks.

Alarmed, Ginger went to her sister-in-law's side. "Felicia love, what's the matter?" Her heart dropped. "Have you heard from Charles?" *If so, the news must be unpleasant.*

"No," Felicia said. "And *that's* the problem. It's like he's never heard of a telephone or a telegram. He's fallen entirely off the map!"

"Oh, darling," Ginger said, patting Felicia's back gently. "He hasn't been gone that long. I'm sure there's a perfectly good reason for his silence. Perhaps he's in the sticks and out of reach of a telephone or telegram station."

Even as the words passed her lips, Ginger heard how they registered falsely. These were modern times. And even if Charles could not avail himself of a telephone, telegram stations were a matter of course.

"I'm going dancing with George Dennison tonight."

"Is that not a rather foolhardy diversion?"

"I'm not waiting around for Charles like a lovesick pigeon. I'm going dancing with George."

The last time Felicia had gone out with George and his ilk, she ended up in the social section of *The Daily News* in a less-than-flattering photograph of her dancing on a tabletop.

Felicia used a linen cloth to clean the black streaks from her cheeks, and after running a tiny flat brush across a mascara pad, she applied a new layer to her eyelashes.

"Are you certain this is the best move, Felicia?" Ginger asked.

"I'm hardly playing a game of chess, Ginger."

"Yes, clearly, but perhaps you shouldn't act rashly. Wait to see what Charles has to say for himself."

Felicia settled on a pair of black T-strap shoes then jumped to her feet. "Why should I?" She stepped in front of the full-length, framed mirror in the corner of the room and admired her selection. "George is fun and *in* London."

"True, but not the sort of gentleman . . ." Ginger used the term loosely, ". . . with whom one can secure a future."

"I'm not looking to secure my future tonight, Ginger. I simply want to have fun." She wrapped a loose string of beads around her neck and whipped the length of it around like a tiny lasso. "After all, I *am* a bright young thing."

"Ambrosia will disapprove."

"She doesn't have to know." Felicia arched one dark, thin brow in Ginger's direction. "You won't tell her, will you?"

"Are you asking me to lie?"

"No, but you needn't go running to her with the news."

"I won't do that. You are a grown woman, Felicia. However, if Ambrosia asks, I'll not tell a falsehood. Where are you going?"

"Ha! Why would I tell you that now?"

"Can I assume I'll find out in the morning rags?"

"Ginger! That was one unfortunate incident that I won't repeat."

"Then," Ginger countered, "in case we need to find you?"

"Fine. We're going to the North Star. All

George's friends shall be there as well as some of mine. Really, Ginger, it's harmless fun."

Acquainted with the club, Ginger had attended it whilst investigating a rather sensitive case.

"I don't suppose anyone from the Lawn Tennis Association frequents that club?" Ginger asked. Nellie Booth and Robert Armstrong were in the same age group as Felicia and her friends.

"On occasion," Felicia said. "Why?"

Ginger relayed the incident with Nellie Booth and her collapse.

"And you believe it to be the work of foul play?"

"Perhaps," Ginger conceded. "The odds that two members of a tennis partnership would be taken out of circulation within a couple of days of each other is rather extreme."

Felicia selected a pretty purple cloche hat and plopped it on her head. "In that case, *Lady Gold*, I'll put my detective cap on. Perhaps my *foolhardy diversion* shall help solve your case."

21

Later that evening—dinner was over, and Felicia had gone—Ginger and Basil could finally relax in the sitting room over a glass of brandy. A customary routine for the couple, they'd get together to share the events of their days. These days, however, Ginger had taken to drinking tonic water with a twist of lime. As she waited, her gaze lingered on *The Mermaid* painting, a Waterhouse, that hung over the stone fireplace. The long red locks of the mythical creature reminded Ginger of her mother, and the painting had been a gift to Mary, her mother, from George Hartigan.

Boss strolled across the jade-coloured Persian carpet and climbed up beside Ginger on the rose-and-saffron-coloured sofa. After being nudged on the arm by his wet nose, Ginger complied with his quiet request for attention by stroking his fur.

"Bossy, I miss you too."

At one time, the little Boston terrier had been her constant companion and closest confidant. After she'd returned to Boston from France without her husband, her father had given the dog to her as a puppy. A poor substitution for Daniel, certainly, but at the time, the puppy had brought her physical and emotional comfort. Over time, Ginger had engaged in life again, and Boss spent more time at home with Scout.

After losing his only living adult relative and having to part with a close cousin, the young lad was charmed by Boss, who gave the boy the companionship he desperately needed. Ginger had been happy to share the little dog with him.

As Basil filled the glasses from the sideboard, kept nicely stocked by Pippins, he said, "Do tell how your tea with the Duchess went?"

"Pleasantly for the most part, but not very revealing. It appears that the Duchess is estranged from her family, her friends too if one can go by Ambrosia's frosty response. But there's nothing that points to Miss Cummings."

Basil strolled to the sofa, handed Ginger her drink, and took a seat beside her.

Ginger asked, "Did you glean anything of interest from Mr. Armstrong?"

"He admitted to having been romantically involved with both Miss Cummings and Miss Booth, regretted each entanglement, but of course, denied any malicious intent. As he was quick to point out, I have no proof, despite weak alibis on both counts."

"Word has it that he's been noted for spending his leisure at the North Star."

Basil stiffened. Memories from a more challenging time were attached to that club, and Ginger hadn't wanted to bring it up.

Basil sipped his drink then said, "Is that where Felicia's gone tonight?"

"Unfortunately, yes. She feels abandoned by Charles and is playing up to lick her wounds." Snuggling close to Basil, Ginger felt his arm gently wrapped around her shoulders. She let out a soft sigh.

"Is everything all right, love?" Basil asked.

Ginger turned to face him. "With all that has happened, I haven't had a chance to tell you."

"Tell me what?" Basil glanced at Ginger's midsection with a look of trepidation.

Ginger hurried to correct his assumption. "Not me; I'm fine. I had a visit from Coco Chanel at my investigations office."

"Oh," Basil let out a breath of relief. "And what did Mademoiselle Chanel have to say."

"She hired me to search out Miss Cummings' killer."

Basil frowned and pulled away. "I thought your interest in the case was out of a sense of duty to me and mutual camaraderie."

"It started that way. But—"

"You realise Miss Chanel is still on my list of suspects. Near the top, in fact."

"And mine too, actually. However, Coco Chanel can be quite persuasive."

"And you, my darling, have never been a pushover."

Basil knows me well, Ginger mused, *for one who doesn't know my whole story*. And she couldn't reveal the reason behind Coco's light touch of blackmail.

"I'm happy to hear you say that," Ginger returned. "As it turns out, I owe Coco a favour, but I was specific in my agreement with her: if I discovered evidence that pointed to her, I would be compelled to deliver it to the police. Unlike her solicitors, I'm not bound by confidentiality."

Basil's shoulders relaxed at that pronouncement, and Ginger was relieved when he pulled her back into himself.

"Very well. We must work together to solve this case; just promise me you'll stay out of harm's way."

"I promise."

The inconspicuous entrance of Pippins followed a tap on the door. "The Earl of Witt, Lord Davenport-Witt, is here."

Oh mercy.

Ginger cast an uneasy glance at Basil before shifting from under his arm and rising to her feet.

"Show him in, Pips."

Seconds later, Charles strolled into the sitting room with his long-legged gait and air of self-importance. "Good evening, Ginger, Basil." He scanned the room, no doubt registering the absence of Felicia, but his expression showed no concern. "Please forgive me for intruding uninvited."

Basil joined Ginger and reached a hand to the earl. "Not at all, old chap. You're always welcome."

Charles gave both Basil and Ginger a hearty handshake.

"That was a quick trip," Ginger said.

"Business," Charles said with a shrug. "There

were people there in desperate need of my autograph." He paused then continued, "I was hoping to find Felicia at home, but alas?"

"I'm afraid she's gone out with friends," Ginger said. "I hope I'm not betraying confidences by saying that Felicia hadn't heard from you and didn't know when to expect you to rejoin our party."

"Yes, well, as I said, I was caught up with business, and truly, time just got away from me. However, you can rest assured that my mind never drifted too far away from our sweet Felicia."

Ginger hummed. "I'm sure she would be flattered."

"Do you know where she's gone?" Charles asked, his eyes flashing with mischief. "I could surprise her. Wouldn't that be jolly good fun?"

Until the earl finds Felicia on the arm of another man, Ginger thought. She must find a way to caution Felicia. She cleared her throat.

"Perhaps you'd like to join us for a drink before you go?" she asked pleasantly. "The night is young."

"Very well." Charles tugged on his trousers before taking a seat then looking to Basil. "Is that brandy, old chap?"

"Indeed."

As Basil returned to the sideboard to pour for their guest, Ginger caught Pippins before he left.

"Pips, would you ring the North Star and ask to send a message to Miss Gold that the earl has arrived in London?"

"Yes, madam. I'll make the call right away."

"Thank you, Pips. I know I can count on you."

Ginger glided back to her place on the sofa, shifting Boss to the spot between her and Basil. She smiled at Charles. "How was France . . . for the short time you were there?"

"Beautiful. Nothing like France in the summer."

Ginger cocked her head. "You sound like you spend a lot of time there."

"Only recently. I've invested in a winery."

"How nice," Ginger said. "One would think a winery would benefit from the installation of a telephone." Her statement had an underlying implication she was certain that, by the flash of acknowledgment in his eyes, Charles understood: He hadn't been gone long enough to have gone to France. So where had he been? Or more precisely, what assignment had the Crown given him?

Charles chuckled in response. "One would think. The French are far more suspicious about modern conveniences. Tradition is everything. I do believe they still make use of the pigeon to relay messages to their customers."

Charles ended his jest with a purposeful sip of brandy, then added, "But enough about my boring business ventures. Do tell, have you found the culprit behind Miss Cummings' demise?"

After a pause, Basil answered. "The investigation is still ongoing."

Charles laughed and lifted his drink. "A fine choice of meaningless words, Chief Inspector."

22

As Basil sat at his desk in his office at Scotland Yard, he heard the familiar, joyous sound of his wife's voice echoing down the hall and smiled.

"Good morning, Officer!"

"Hello, Mrs. Reed," the desk clerk said. "Fine day, isn't it?"

"Yes, lovely," Ginger agreed. "Is the chief inspector in his office?"

"Yes, madam, he is."

"Thank you, Officer."

Basil tidied his desktop as he anticipated Ginger's soft knock.

"Basil, love," she said. "Can you spare a few minutes?"

"Anything for you, my dear."

Basil watched with admiration as Ginger, dressed elegantly in a pretty summer frock, gracefully took a seat on the wooden chair opposite his desk. She crossed her legs and pulled at the fingertips of her gloves, a common course of action that she somehow made sophisticated. Though he'd seen her just a few hours earlier over a shared breakfast, he never tired of gazing upon her beauty, much like a schoolboy with a tremendous crush on someone far out of reach.

However, he had got the girl and never, for an instant, took his good fortune for granted.

"Ginger!" he said, forcing himself to keep an air of professionalism. "Have you news?"

Ginger neatly placed her gloves on his desk. "I'm not sure. I feel like the edges of the puzzle are fuzzy, and perhaps if we reviewed the clues together . . ."

Basil opened his desk drawer and removed a file. "I've meant to show you these. They're the police photographs from the afternoon of the murder."

Basil handed Ginger the file, and she perused the photos.

"Well?" Basil said.

"Not a lot here that we didn't see with our own eyes."

Basil sighed. "That was my conclusion too."

"But," Ginger said, her luscious lips—shiny with red lipstick—working. "Have you contacted the press? Perhaps Mr. Brown captured something inadvertently."

"Good idea," Basil said. "He's with *The Daily News*, isn't he?"

"Yes," Ginger confirmed.

Just as Basil pulled the black telephone closer, it rang. He glanced at Ginger with a look of surprise before picking up the handpiece from the telephone cradle. "Reed here."

Covering the mouthpiece, he whispered, "Speak of the devil." Then, into the receiver, he said, "Hello, Mr. Brown. Uh-huh, uh-huh. Strangely enough, my wife and I were just speaking about that very thing. Yes, we'll meet you there."

Ginger raised a brow at Basil as he hung up the telephone.

Basil reached for his hat. "Mr. Brown has photographs. He wants to meet us in Hyde Park."

BASIL DROVE towards the scene of the crime with Ginger in the passenger seat of his Austin. "How are you feeling, love?" In the light of day, he'd noticed evidence of shadows under her eyes. "You look a little peaked."

As if triggered by the suggestion, Ginger raised a gloved hand to her lips to suppress a yawn. "I'm a little tired. But not so much that I can't do this. I'll rest later."

Basil laid a gentle hand on Ginger's arm. His wife was strong but not invincible, and he couldn't help the pang of worry that wound about his heart. "You'll promise not to overdo things?"

"I promise. I've done nothing more than talk today. Hardly overexertion."

"I'll drive you home after this."

"But my motorcar is at the Yard."

"Not to worry, my dear. I'll have it driven to our house."

"In normal circumstances, I'd argue with you, but I am feeling rather weary."

Basil manoeuvred through a mix of motorised machines and horses, eventually entering the park at Wellington Arch.

Blake Brown had beaten them there. He leaned against the rail of the now-empty gazebo. With the tents, runway, and chairs gone, the park looked docile and peaceful, with people languidly strolling along the paths and picnickers dotting the areas of the lawn where the sheep had recently grazed.

"One would never guess that a murder had occurred here a short while ago," Ginger said.

Blake Brown descended the gazebo steps when he saw them and approached. A round of handshaking occurred, then Basil asked, "What do you have, Mr. Brown, and why bring us here?"

"I think you'll understand when you see this photograph. I didn't know when I was snapping what I had captured, and I only got the chance to develop the plates this morning."

The journalist removed a large envelope from his satchel, removed a print, and handed it to Basil.

Ginger let out a small gasp as Basil low-whistled. The image was slightly blurry but clearly captured when the dart had embedded itself in Miss Cummings neck just before she fell. She must've pulled it out and released it, which was why Basil had found it in the grass.

Ginger immediately walked to the area of the lawn the runway had covered. "Miss Cummings was about here when she was struck?"

Thankfully, Basil had thought to bring his folder of photographs. One of them was a distance shot after the crowd had been dispersed, but the body was still on the runway. He compared Ginger's position to the photograph.

"Take another step towards the gazebo."

Ginger did so, and Basil nodded. "Yes, that's the spot."

Basil squinted at the dart in Mr. Brown's photograph. "The shooter of the dart had to have concealed himself somewhere." He glanced at the grouping of trees in the park. "A tree would be a natural choice, but there aren't any near the runway or behind the seated crowd. None close enough to offer concealment, and yet, the shorter distance needed to blow a dart or throw it by hand."

"With Mr. Brown's photograph," Ginger started, "we can determine the direction the dart travelled."

"North-east," the journalist volunteered. "Depending on how far the dart travelled, it would've been shot from approximately—" Mr. Brown took long strides in a north-easterly direction then stopped. "—here."

Basil and Ginger shared a serious look. Mr. Brown stood in the exact location where Coco Chanel's tent had been set up.

"Where was Mademoiselle Chanel when Miss Tatum and Miss Cummings fell?" Basil asked.

Ginger shook her head. "Felicia's fall had everyone's attention. Everyone's focus was on that, not the area behind them

Basil paced as he scanned the area. "Did you notice if the designer was seated?"

Ginger placed a finger on her chin. "My gaze was trained on Felicia and Millie, but I did glance at the seated designers if only to see if their faces and expressions betrayed their thoughts regarding Emma's designs. I'm quite certain I saw an empty chair."

"Had Mademoiselle Chanel left her seat?" Basil asked. "I know you're trying to prove her innocence, but we have to follow the evidence, love."

"I believe so; Coco insists that nature had called, and she had to find a lavatory. Still, what we have is circumstantial."

At that moment, Braxton ran towards them. "Chief Inspector!"

Basil had left word at the Yard as to where he was headed, so it wasn't surprising that Braxton had located him there. The question was, why?

"What is it, Braxton?"

"Mademoiselle Chanel's parasol, sir. One of the men found it in a rubbish bin."

Ginger stared in dismay. "Are you certain?"

"It fits the description, madam," Braxton said.

"And it was disassembled. The bamboo shaft separated from the parasol."

Basil turned to Ginger. "She did say it was unique. At least until production in China started. I'm afraid I'm going to have to bring her and her assistant in."

Ginger's green eyes flashed with deeper fatigue. "Oh mercy."

23

Ginger's desire for a lie down would have to wait a bit longer. Instead, she was back at Scotland Yard with an irate client sitting in Basil's office.

"This is outrageous!" Coco said, her dark eyes flashing between Basil, who sat behind his desk, and Ginger, on a second, matching chair to the side. "I demand that you release Jean-Luc immediately!"

"He is being held for questioning," Basil said calmly. "As hard as it must be to hear, Mr. Marchand is our prime suspect in the death of Irene Cummings."

"Why is that?" Coco demanded.

Ginger explained, "If one used the hollow bamboo shaft of your parasol to shoot the dart, one would have to blow with extraordinary strength. It leads us to conclude that a man is most likely the perpetrator. Evidence leads to your tent as the point of origin."

Coco shrugged. "Bad publicity is as good as good publicity, and once word of this gets out, sales of my parasol will skyrocket."

"You do realise, Coco," Ginger said, "you've just pronounced your motive."

The designer blinked, and for a moment, a look of uncertainty flashed behind her dark eyes. "You do not seriously consider *me* a suspect."

"It's your parasol," Basil said. "You and Mr. Marchand could've planned the attack together."

"That is preposterous. Anyone could have had access to the parasol. It is not as if those tents were secured. And what would I, or Jean-Luc, have against a common tennis player?"

"That's what we'll have to find out," Basil said. "Our laboratory has examined the hollow bamboo shaft, and human spittle was found inside."

Coco harrumphed. "There is no way to prove to whom the spittle belongs. Did you at least find fingerprints?"

"Only your own," Ginger provided. Coco Chanel had been indignant when requested to ink her fingertips. Thankfully, the ink could be removed with a clean cloth and rubbing alcohol.

"Of course mine would be on it! It was my parasol."

"Mademoiselle Chanel," Basil began, "we have proof that the trajectory of the dart came from the direction of your tent."

Coco scoffed. "The responsibility was not mine. And it could not have been Jean-Luc."

"How do you know?" Ginger asked.

"Because I know Jean-Luc. He would not hurt a fly. Now, if we are finished, I must return to my house and ring my solicitor."

"You may go," Basil said. "But please, don't leave London."

If looks could kill, Ginger believed that she and Basil would most certainly be dead. Coco Chanel stormed out of the office like a tempest.

"I'd hate to get on her bad side," Basil said with a wry grin.

"I'm afraid we're already on her bad side, love."

Basil leaned back in his chair and rubbed his chin. "Why don't you go on home now? I'll wrap things up here and meet you for dinner."

Ginger was very happy to agree to Basil's suggestion. Nothing more was going to get between her and her pillow!

But alas, just as Ginger had settled into her bed, comfortably under silk sheets with Boss curled up beside her, a tap on her bedroom door was followed by a bedraggled-looking Felicia, who dragged herself in and flopped into one of the striped upholstered chairs near the tall window.

"Bossy," Ginger said playfully. "Look at what the cat's dragged in."

Felicia moaned.

Ginger shifted into a sitting position and stroked Boss' soft fur. "Rough night, last night, I gather?"

"I fear I had one too many cocktails. And did you know that Charles had the nerve to turn up! How did he even know I was there?" Felicia's eyes narrowed. "Of course, you must've told him."

"He asked. You never said it was a secret." Ginger felt a modicum of regret. "I thought you'd be pleased."

"George, that blasted idiot, decided to take liberties just as Charles walked into the room."

"Liberties?"

"He kissed me, and I can assure you that I did not kiss him in return."

"What happened?"

Felicia's lips twitched, and a look of mischief flashed behind her eyes. "Charles popped him one on the nose."

"Oh mercy. Then what happened?"

"He was very cross with me, even though I was the *kissed,* not the *kisser.* But I was cross with him too. He neither owns me nor gets to decide who I kiss."

"I see. Are things over between you then?" Ginger couldn't say that she'd be all that troubled by the news, but Ambrosia would be crushed.

"Oh no. Charles is taking me out for dinner tonight. He reassured me that I was the only one he cared about, so I've decided to forgive him. Oh—" Felicia sat upright. "I've just remembered. I learned something about Irene Cummings."

"Oh?" Ginger's attention was stoked afresh. "What's that?"

"George said she was expecting a child."

Ginger frowned. "How would he know that?"

"Irene was a confidante of his sister."

"Did she reveal who the father was?"

"Well, she was most recently connected to Robert Armstrong. Perhaps it was him?"

Ginger hummed. Mr. Armstrong had just raced back to the top of her suspect list.

"I need to find something to wear," Felicia said, suddenly in buoyed spirits. "Ginger, could I borrow your little black Chanel dress? Charles will go mad!"

"Of course."

Ginger slunk under the covers as she watched Felicia playfully model the black chiffon dress with its low waist, flouncy skirt, and gold-lace-trimmed deep V-neckline. "You look lovely," she muttered, before slipping into sleep.

24

The next morning, Ginger headed to her study at the back of the house. Boss, behind her, created rapid clicking sounds on the tiles with his nails. Originally her father's workplace, Ginger had kept the dark, masculine tones in memory of him, replacing only the oversized, topple-prone office chair for something more modern and suitable for her size. The walls were ceiling-to-floor shelves, holding leather-bound albums of George Hartigan's favourite tomes, fiction and otherwise. A stone fireplace, now empty of embers, took up one wall. On the burgundy wallpaper next to the fireplace, a large portrait of a young George Hartigan hung. A red and blue Turkish carpet took up most of the floor, and the heels of Ginger's Italian-leather pumps were silent as she approached the big wooden desk.

Taking her place in the chair, Ginger reviewed her mail, realising with a start she was behind on her correspondence for Feathers & Flair and her part in the failed fashion show. There were invoices to pay, rental items to ensure were returned, and of course, designers to appease, all of whom were unhappy with having to remain captive in London.

Using the black typewriter, Ginger composed a letter to the editor of *The Daily News*, hoping that a reassuring statement to the public would ease any fears and encourage the city planners to endorse future fashion events. The death of Miss Irene Cummings was unfortunate, but violence was not a typical occurrence in the fashion world.

Just as she got to the end of the letter, Boss nudged her elbow.

"Hey, Bossy."

Her pet licked her hand and attempted, but failed, to jump onto her lap. Ginger offered assistance and said with a giggle, "I'm afraid another is vying for space here. Won't be long, and there won't be any room for you."

Boss whined and nosed her belly.

"It'll be fine, Boss," she said as she rubbed the

base of his pointy ears. "Just like when Scout came to us. There's always enough love to go around."

Ginger's ornate telephone rang with its pleasant jingle. Hartigan House had a house telephone, naturally, but Ginger had been fortunate to secure a second line for business use. A rather decadent coup, she thought, as most citizens of the British Isles did not even have one. The British consensus was that if you needed to contact someone, the post, which arrived at private residences several times a day, was enough. No one needed immediate contact!

Ginger picked up the black and gold receiver. "Good morning, Mrs. Reed speaking."

"Hello, love."

Ginger perked up at the sound of her husband's smooth voice. "Basil? Is everything all right?"

"Perfectly, thank you. I just wanted to let you know that I've heard from Dr. Wood. He's completed the post-mortem and suggested I go to see him."

"And you're inviting me to join you!"

"Of course. We may be working for different parties, but we desire the same outcome."

"The truth about how and why Miss Cummings died."

"Precisely."

"I'm on my way."

"Drive carefully."

"I shall."

"I mean it, Ginger."

"As do I." Puzzled, Ginger set the receiver back on its cradle. Why was everyone always so concerned about her driving? A few mishaps, kerb-cutting, and horn-honking weren't that big a deal.

SHE SUCCESSFULLY ARRIVED at University College Hospital—well, with only *one* rather large bump from hitting a pothole on her way. Sure, she'd admit it would've been fitting for her to slow down a bit...

Ginger stood on the pavement at the entrance. Having been to this mortuary numerous times, she knew the lie of the land. Like most mortuaries, this one was below ground, and she took the steps down. Before entering, she knocked on the white door, and found Dr. Wood and Basil standing in the middle of the white room—the scent of a mix of lemon cleaner and formaldehyde, burning her nose. The men encircled the ceramic slab that held Miss Cummings' body.

Ginger had seen more than her fair share of corpses in her lifetime, as had most people who'd spent time on the continent during the war. Irene Cummings' nude body was covered to the shoulders by a white sheet, her arms exposed at her side. Her face, very pale and tinged with blue, was unmarred and relaxed. A red puncture wound on her neck stood out against the backdrop of white skin.

"Good morning," Ginger said as she entered.

"Fine day, Mrs. Reed," Dr. Wood countered. The pathologist was a very pale specimen, perhaps due to spending little time in the sun. At least his lips were rosy and his eyes bright, signs he was indeed alive and not the walking dead.

"Dr. Wood was just about to review his report," Basil said.

Dr. Wood retrieved a pair of spectacles from his white surgical smock's chest pocket and put them on.

"The deceased was in above-average physical health, which lines up with her athletic nature. All the organs were extracted and weighed, and no abnormalities were determined."

"Was she with child?" Ginger asked.

Basil shot her a look.

Dr. Wood stared over his spectacles. "As a matter of fact, she was."

Basil cast Ginger a surprised look. "How did you know?"

"Felicia's acquaintance, who's George's sister, was a friend of Irene's."

"Really," Basil said with a note of amusement. "Can I presume her condition came as a result of her liaison with Mr. Armstrong?"

"That's my assumption." Ginger turned back to Dr. Wood. "Do you know what killed Miss Cummings?"

"Yes. She was poisoned. At first, I was perplexed as I couldn't narrow the poison down to the usual culprits, and then I conferred with a colleague who has spent a considerable amount of time abroad." Mr. Wood removed his spectacles then continued, "He said it sounds like the poison extracted from the skin of the dart frogs, a species typically found in rainforests in South America and used for hunting by the indigenous people there."

Ginger caught Basil's eye. Together they said, "Nellie Booth."

25

Ginger and Basil raced for the door.

"She's in a ward on the second floor," Ginger said.

"I'm going to sprint, love," Basil said. "I'll meet you there."

Ginger couldn't blame Basil for his hurry, and in her current condition, not to mention her day frock and heels, she could hardly expect to keep up.

As she headed up the stairs, she thought about Nellie Booth. Ambitious and competitive, the tennis player had her eyes set on being the best female tennis star in London. Had she been threatened by Irene Cummings' ranking?

Nellie Booth had recently returned from Brazil where this poison quite possibly had its origins, and

Ginger couldn't think of another person who could have had access to the substance. They had been wrong in their initial assumptions that the killer had to be male. A woman with strong lungs, say, developed in the frequent play of aerobic games such as tennis, could have accomplished the dart-blowing stunt.

The question was, how had she known Coco Chanel would arrive with the bamboo parasol?

Ginger herself was blessed with natural athleticism and, despite her delicate condition, made it to the second floor of the hospital in good time and not excessively out of breath. She ran to the open door of Nellie Booth's ward to find Basil staring despondently at an empty bed.

"She's gone," he said.

Ginger took in the crumpled bedsheets. "She can't have been gone long. The nurses haven't changed the bedding. Are you certain she's not just gone to the loo or taken a stroll around the ward?"

A rather haggard-looking nurse bustled into the room. "I'm sorry, Chief Inspector, but it appears that her day clothes are gone. I fear she left without being discharged by her doctor. We're very worried, sir. Dr. Shaw has just diagnosed her with paranoia as a result of drug use."

Ginger wondered if drug use was to blame for Nellie's fainting episode after her tennis game.

"Thank you, Nurse Walker," Basil said. "Please report Miss Booth's departure to your superiors."

Basil turned to Ginger. "I'm going to ring the Yard for constable support and then search about the hospital and grounds."

Ginger nodded. "I'll have a chat with the doctor."

Ginger found a grouping of agitated nurses at the nurses' station, white headscarves perfectly affixed with hairgrips. They looked perplexed and dismayed.

At one end of the long counter, Basil held a telephone receiver to one ear and a palm to the other to hear over the cacophony of voices.

Ginger spoke loudly, "Where might I find Dr. Shaw?"

A male voice broke through. "I'm here."

"Miss Booth appears to have left the hospital," Nurse Walker said.

Ginger reached out a gloved hand to the doctor. "I'm Mrs. Reed of Lady Gold Investigations, and I consult with Scotland Yard—"

"Oh, yes, I've heard of you, Mrs. Reed," the

doctor said, cautiously. "But I'm in the middle of a situation here. Perhaps you can come back later."

Having dismissed her, the doctor turned his back. Ginger nudged his elbow. "It's about Miss Booth that I'm enquiring, Dr. Shaw. She's a prime suspect in a murder investigation."

"Then why am I not speaking to the police?"

"The police are on their way, I assure you." She pointed to where Basil had been standing, but he was gone. "I only want to know if you believe that Miss Booth, in her current mental state, could be a danger to herself or others."

Dr. Shaw huffed. "I believe she may. I was about to have a psychiatrist analyse her. I suppose I was remiss in relaying my intentions to the patient."

"I presume you're aware that Miss Booth had problems with alcohol," Ginger began, "Do you know if she struggled with other substances?"

After a short nod, the doctor said, "At first I suspected opium use as she was beginning to show typical signs of withdrawal, but the results of her blood test have just come in—"

"And?" Ginger prompted.

With reluctance, the doctor finished his sentence. "There was a good amount of cannabis in her blood stream."

"Do you have any idea where she might've gone? Anything she may have said that might indicate a possibility?"

The doctor shook his head. "I'm sorry. Now, if you'll please excuse me."

When the physician was out of earshot, Nurse Walker touched Ginger's arm. "Miss Booth said something in my hearing, madam."

"Did she?"

"I thought it was delirium talking, but she mentioned a man in unkind terms. She said she hated him and would kill him next."

Ginger leaned in. "Do you recall the man's name?"

"Hmm, Robert something. Strong?

"Armstrong?"

"Yes." The nurse snapped her fingers. "That's it."

26

*A*s providence would have it, Robert Armstrong had once been admitted to University College Hospital, and Nurse Walker retrieved his home address for Ginger. Unable to locate Basil, Ginger turned to the nurse behind the counter. "Please ring up Scotland Yard and leave a message for Chief Inspector Basil Reed. Let the officer you speak to know that I'm on my way to Mr. Armstrong's house and that the police should attend as soon as possible."

Nurse Walker had the telephone receiver in her hand before the words had left Ginger's mouth, a sign of her efficiency and competence, despite the disappearance of one of her patients.

Ginger's Crossley never disappointed, and in her

speedy fashion, she breezed through busy crossroads. She dodged horses drawing carts laden with various wares, wooden double-decker buses painted pillar-box red, and sensible pedestrians, who darted to safety onto pavements. Drivers inexplicably reached out of their windows to squeeze the rubber ball of their brass horns, and Ginger, sorely tempted, once did the same in return. She came to a rather sudden stop in front of Mr. Armstrong's residence, a black cat wisely climbing a nearby tree.

Propriety insisted that Ginger knock before entering, but her gloved fist paused mid-air before contacting the wooden door. A scuffling sound on the other side caused her to reach into her handbag for her pistol with one hand and turn the knob with the other.

Mr. Armstrong lived in a large flat with no interior walls. *Rather bohemian*, Ginger thought with a flash of surprise. The interior was dotted with mismatched furnishings, now being used by Mr. Armstrong as barriers to attack.

Miss Booth lifted a long pipe-like device to her lips and blew. Mr. Armstrong leapt over the sofa which flipped onto its side and concealed him from his attacker. A dart stuck into a wooden beam on the wall.

"Miss Booth!" Ginger called.

Nellie Booth turned at the sound of her name and furrowed her brow in confusion. "Mrs. Reed?"

Robert Armstrong's head bobbed up from behind the sofa's edge. "Thank God! Get help! This madwoman is trying to kill me!"

Nellie stared blankly. "Oh yes, that's right, I was."

From the pocket of her skirt, she retrieved another dart.

Ginger lifted her pistol. "Miss Booth, I implore you to put your weapon down."

Nellie pouted. "He didn't even visit me in hospital."

Robert Armstrong made an error in judgement and stood to his defence. "Dash it all! It's not like you're my sweetheart."

"Irene was going to trap you with that baby and make you marry her!"

"She didn't deserve to die!"

"I fixed things for you, Robert," Nellie pouted, "because I love you. And this is the thanks I get?" She loaded the dart into the pipe and blew it. Robert Armstrong dived for cover, missing impalement by a fraction of an inch.

Ginger held the Remington with both hands,

arms outstretched and feet braced. "Miss Booth! Drop your weapon, or you'll force me to shoot you."

Eyes glazed over as if she wasn't registering reality, Nellie Booth removed another dart from her frock. "Oh, blast it. My last one."

"Nellie!" Ginger admonished.

Nellie's lip lifted at one corner as she held the pipe to her mouth, aiming it this time at Ginger. "We'll have a duel, shall we?"

Ginger's spine tingled with chills. Nellie Booth was not in her right mind, and she was, at this moment, pointing a charged weapon in Ginger's direction. Ginger's heart sank knowing that should Miss Booth shoot her, the dart would hit her straight in the stomach, directly over her growing child. That left only one option, and that was to shoot the troubled girl in self-defence.

"Please, Miss Booth," Ginger said smoothly. "I beseech you. Let us not duel but shake hands as friends."

Nellie lowered the pipe and tilted her head. "All right."

Ginger felt her body flood with relief as she slowly lowered her weapon. "Please give me the blow dart, Nellie."

"Yes, madam," Nellie said.

Then as quick as a whistle, she pivoted and blew. The dart whizzed across the room towards Robert, who'd been quietly making his escape.

He didn't quite make it.

Ginger groaned. The dart hit Mr. Armstrong firmly in his right buttock.

Mr. Armstrong dropped to the floor, groaning.

Oh mercy!

"Mr. Armstrong?" Keeping one eye on Nellie, Ginger ran to the fallen man's side.

He pulled the dart out of his backside. "I hope that fool of a woman didn't poison me."

Ginger had the same concern, but Robert Armstrong looked more embarrassed than poisoned. She held up two fingers.

"How many fingers do you see, Mr. Armstrong?"

"Two."

Nellie Booth flopped onto the only upright chair and sighed. "I ran out of froggie poison." Her eyes glistened as if falling into a memory. "They're such pretty little things. Shiny blood red and deep blue."

Ginger gently guided the pipe out of Nellie's hand. "You must've been very quick to get this from your flat after leaving hospital."

"I'm an athlete, madam. Running isn't hard for me."

Ginger righted the neighbouring chair and sat, her gun clasped in one hand, but resting in her lap, just in case. "Tell me more about the froggie poison, Nellie."

"Oh, it's spectacular stuff. My uncle knows all about the Brazilian tribes and how they use the poison from these little tree frogs to hunt larger game. He let me try it out, though, sadly, I wasn't very good. I just had to sneak a bit back to England with me."

Her head relaxed against the back of the chair as she continued, "Everyone is so relaxed over there. We spent every evening smoking *weed*. That's slang for cannabis, if you weren't aware." Her eyes darted to Ginger. "Now don't be shocked! I know it's not a very ladylike thing to do, especially for us English ladies, but in the Brazilian jungle, there wasn't anyone about to tell one what one could and could not do."

In the background, Ginger heard sirens. Moments later, the sound of quick and heavy steps on the stairs were followed by Basil, springing into the room. His gaze dropped to the pistol in Ginger's hand.

"Ginger!"

"I'm all right, Basil. But we need an ambulance

for Mr. Armstrong." She nodded towards the man sitting up against the wall, wincing in his discomfort. "Miss Booth shot him in the, er, behind. And she'll need a lift back to the hospital. She's definitely unwell."

27

Two weeks later, a judge declared Nellie Booth unfit for trial and sent her to Broadmoor, the hospital for the criminally insane. Ginger did feel sorry for the tennis player because her trip to Brazil, which was meant to be an adventure with only memories and souvenirs brought home, had turned into something so dark and deadly. A new blood test had confirmed the presence of a sativa cannabis strain from South America known to cause paranoia in some of its users. That explained the sweet, smoky smell Ginger had detected in Miss Booth's presence, and her unhinged behaviour. That, and the fact that Ginger had seen her sneaking alcohol at the fashion show, would point to an abuse of other substances.

However, Nellie Booth's state of mind couldn't excuse what must've been a premeditated plan cooked up weeks before. Miss Booth's resentment towards Irene Cummings had run deep. Coco Chanel arriving at the fashion show with her bamboo parasol created an opportunity of passion for Nellie, who at the time had been inebriated and not thinking clearly. One might conclude that this new parasol could be dismantled much like any other. And if her performance with Mr. Armstrong was anything to go by, Nellie's talent for tennis didn't extend to darts. Millie and Felicia became collateral damage as she aimed at Miss Cummings, her true target.

Ginger could only hope that the tragedy would shake the rogue Mr. Armstrong into a state of sober responsibility and that in the future, he'd be far more careful when engaging with the fairer sex.

Coco Chanel had paid Ginger for her work, having had her name cleared and, inadvertently, sales of her now-infamous parasol boosted. All the designers were relieved to be released. Coco had promised to contact Ginger when she returned from Paris, inviting her to tea.

Perhaps the two would become genuine friends one day, after all.

Ginger was pleased to have her family life and her work routines return to normal. Madame Roux ran Feathers & Flair like a well-oiled machine, and Felicia—now happily reunited with Charles and all misunderstandings swept away—worked on her latest mystery manuscript from the offices of Lady Gold Investigations. No new clients had ventured in or rung, and Ginger was satisfied with the lull, preferring to keep her feet up as she read a book in the sitting room and having more time to lounge about with Basil when he was home.

Boss, who kept her company if Scout was engaged with his tutor, had become adept at telling the time. The clock on the mantel struck the hour, and he rose from his doggy bed, shook himself awake, and walked out. Scout's lessons had ended.

Ginger smiled. She roused herself as well, remembering a letter in her study from her American half-sister, Louisa, that needed answering.

Ginger heard voices coming from the drawing room on the opposite side as she stepped into the hall. One of the double wooden doors had been left ajar.

"Really, Ambrosia, you are impossible."

Ginger ducked her chin in shock. The voice was

elderly and female and most certainly sounded like the Duchess of Worthington. She stepped quietly to the doorway to confirm her suspicions.

"I'm not sure what it is that you want from me, Deborah," Ambrosia returned. "You betrayed the sisterhood."

"*Betrayal* is a very strong word. How about a measure of understanding? If anyone should understand, it's you."

Ginger stared through the opening to see the two ladies sitting in matching green-velvet pincushion chairs, hugging the fireplace. A baby grand piano sat in the corner behind them.

"I'm sorry that your marriage to the Duke isn't to your satisfaction, but I'm afraid that doesn't change anything," Ambrosia said coolly.

The Duchess shot to her feet. "Well, if that's the way you feel, I'll find my way out."

Ginger darted away from the doors, not wanting to be caught eavesdropping. It was unbecoming behaviour, but Ginger blamed the war and her spy training for making her so curious and careful about everything.

She made it to the staircase before the Duchess stormed out, and she pretended to be on the first step on her way up. She feigned surprise. "Your Grace!"

The Duchess' surprise wasn't put on. "Oh, Mrs. Reed. Do forgive me. I've been to visit the Dowager Lady Gold. I'm just taking my leave."

Ginger stepped in beside the Duchess. "How delightful. Where is Ambrosia now?"

"She's, er, fatigued, so I offered to show myself out."

"Well, I insist on walking you to your driver. I assume he's waiting outside?"

"Of course."

Ginger struggled to find a way to bring up the rift between the Duchess and Ambrosia without it being obvious that she'd just overheard their disagreement. As she opened the front doors, she said, "How nice it is that the two of you could renew your friendship after so many years."

"Yes, well . . ." The Duchess left her thought unfinished.

They reached the Duchess' motorcar, and the driver jumped out to open the back door for her.

The Duchess glanced at Ginger with regret flashing behind tired eyes. "Good day, Mrs. Reed."

"Good day, Your Grace."

Had Ginger known that would be the last conversation she would have with the Duchess, she would've asked more questions, especially about this mysterious "sisterhood".

What would it take to get Ambrosia to open up? Though the dowager enjoyed a bit of gossip now and again, she could be tighter than a clam when it came to her own secrets.

And as for secrets, Ginger had plenty of her own. She stepped back inside, just as Ambrosia neared the top of the stairs. The dowager looked rather older than she had that morning. Whatever her past with the Duchess, it wasn't something to be ignored.

"Grandmother," Ginger called out. "Is everything all right? I just walked the Duchess of Worthington to her motorcar, and she seemed unsettled."

"I'm fine and she's fine and it's none of anyone's business." Ambrosia picked up her skirt and banged her walking stick rather loudly down the corridor to her room. Though prickly by nature, Ambrosia's abrupt statement was rude, even for her.

Ginger sighed. Her natural inquisitiveness was a tremendous trait when it came to her investigative work, but when it came to Ambrosia, her curiosity would have to wait.

If you enjoyed reading *Murder in Hyde Park* please help others enjoy it too.

Recommend it: Help others find the book by recommending it to friends, readers' groups, discussion boards and by **suggesting it to your local library.**

Review it: Please tell other readers why you liked this book by reviewing it on Amazon or Goodreads.

* No spoilers please *

Don't miss the next Ginger Gold mystery~
MURDER AT ROYAL ALBERT HALL

Murder makes a scene!

Nothing ruins a night of Shakespeare faster than a duchess falling to her death. Mrs. Ginger Reed, also known by some as Lady Gold, is at the Royal Albert Hall with her husband, Basil Reed, a chief inspector at Scotland Yard, and the two of them are immediately at the scene. Was the duchess of Worthington's fall accidental? Where was the duke?

And what does Ginger's grandmother, Ambrosia, the dowager Lady Gold have to do with the sordid affair?

Something went terribly wrong with the dowager's "sisterhood" of friends back in the 1860s, and it's all coming home to roost.

Buy on AMAZON or read Free with Kindle Unlimited!

~

Have you discovered Rosa Reed?
Check out this new, fun 1950s cozy mystery series!

MURDER AT HIGH TIDE
a Rosa Reed Mystery #1

Murder's all wet!

It's 1956 and WPC (Woman Police Constable) Rosa Reed has left her groom at the altar in London. Time spent with her American cousins in Santa Bonita, California is exactly what she needs to get back on her feet, though the last thing she expected was to get entangled in another murder case!

If you love early rock & roll, poodle skirts,

clever who-dun-its, a charming cat and an even more charming detective, you're going to love this new series!

Buy on AMAZON or read Free with Kindle Unlimited!

GINGER GOLD'S JOURNAL

Sign up for Lee's readers list and gain access to **Ginger Gold's private Journal.** Find out about Ginger's Life before the SS *Rosa* and how she became the woman she has. This is a fluid document that will cover her romance with her late husband Daniel, her time serving in the British secret service during World War One, and beyond. Includes a recipe for Dark Dutch Chocolate Cake!

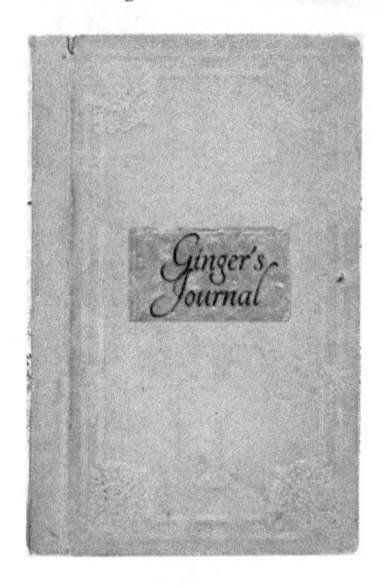

It begins: **July 31, 1912**

How fabulous that I found this Journal today, hidden in the bottom of my wardrobe. Good old Pippins, our English butler in London, gave it to me as a parting gift when Father whisked me away on our American adventure so he could marry Sally. Pips said it was for me to record my new adventures. I'm ashamed I never even penned one word before today. I think I was just too sad.

This old leather-bound journal takes me back to that emotional time. I had shed enough tears to fill the ocean and I remember telling

Father dramatically that I was certain to cause flooding to match God's. At eight years old I was well-trained in my biblical studies, though, in retro-spect, I would say that I had probably bordered on heresy with my little tantrum.

The first week of my "adventure" was spent with a tummy ache and a number of embarrassing sessions that involved a bucket and Father holding back my long hair so I wouldn't soil it with vomit.

I certainly felt that I was being punished for some reason. Hartigan House—though large and sometimes lonely—was my home and Pips was my good friend. He often helped me to pass the time with games of I Spy and Xs and Os.

"Very good, Little Miss," he'd say with a twinkle in his blue eyes when I won, which I did often. I suspect now that our good butler wasn't beyond letting me win even when unmerited.

Father had got it into his silly head that I needed a mother, but I think the truth was he wanted a wife. Sally, a woman half my father's age, turned out to be a sufficient wife in the end, but I could never claim her as a mother.

Well, Pips, I'm sure you'd be happy to know that things turned out all right here in America.

SUBSCRIBE to read more!

http://www.leestraussbooks.com/gingergoldjournalsignup/

ABOUT THE AUTHOR

Lee Strauss is a USA TODAY bestselling author of The Ginger Gold Mysteries series, The Higgins & Hawke Mystery series, The Rosa Reed Mystery series (cozy historical mysteries), A Nursery Rhyme Mystery series (mystery suspense), The Perception series (young adult dystopian), The Light & Love series (sweet romance), The Clockwise Collection (YA time travel romance), and young adult historical fiction with over a million books read. She has titles published in German, Spanish and Korean, and a growing audio library.

When Lee's not writing or reading she likes to cycle, hike, and stare at the ocean. She loves to drink caffè lattes and red wines in exotic places, and eat dark chocolate anywhere.

For more info on books by Lee Strauss and her social media links, visit leestraussbooks.com. To make sure you don't miss the next new release, be sure to sign up for her readers' list!

www.leestraussbooks.com
leestraussbooks@gmail.com

MORE FROM LEE STRAUSS

On AMAZON

GINGER GOLD MYSTERY SERIES (cozy 1920s historical)

Cozy. Charming. Filled with Bright Young Things. This Jazz Age murder mystery will entertain and delight you with its 1920s flair and pizzazz!

Murder on the SS Rosa

Murder at Hartigan House

Murder at Bray Manor

Murder at Feathers & Flair

Murder at the Mortuary

Murder at Kensington Gardens

Murder at St. George's Church

The Wedding of Ginger & Basil

Murder Aboard the Flying Scotsman

Murder at the Boat Club

Murder on Eaton Square

Murder by Plum Pudding

Murder on Fleet Street

Murder at Brighton Beach

Murder in Hyde Park

Murder at the Royal Albert Hall

Murder in Belgravia

LADY GOLD INVESTIGATES (Ginger Gold companion short stories)

Volume 1

Volume 2

Volume 3

Volume 4

HIGGINS & HAWKE MYSTERY SERIES (cozy 1930s historical)

The 1930s meets Rizzoli & Isles in this friendship depression era cozy mystery series.

Death at the Tavern

Death on the Tower

Death on Hanover

THE ROSA REED MYSTERIES

(1950s cozy historical)

Murder at High Tide

Murder on the Boardwalk

Murder at the Bomb Shelter

Murder on Location

Murder and Rock 'n Roll

Murder at the Races

Murder at the Dude Ranch

A NURSERY RHYME MYSTERY SERIES (mystery/sci fi)

Marlow finds himself teamed up with intelligent and savvy Sage Farrell, a girl so far out of his league he feels blinded in her presence - literally - damned glasses! Together they work to find the identity of @gingerbreadman. Can they stop the killer before he strikes again?

Gingerbread Man

Life Is but a Dream

Hickory Dickory Dock

Twinkle Little Star

THE PERCEPTION TRILOGY (YA dystopian

mystery)

Zoe Vanderveen is a GAP—a genetically altered person. She lives in the security of a walled city on prime water-front property along side other equally beautiful people with extended life spans. Her brother Liam is missing. Noah Brody, a boy on the outside, is the only one who can help ∼ but can she trust him?

Perception

Volition

Contrition

LIGHT & LOVE (sweet romance)

Set in the dazzling charm of Europe, follow Katja, Gabriella, Eva, Anna and Belle as they find strength, hope and love.

Sing me a Love Song

Your Love is Sweet

In Light of Us

Lying in Starlight

PLAYING WITH MATCHES (WW2 history/romance)

A sobering but hopeful journey about how one young German boy copes with the war and propaganda. Based on true events.

A Piece of Blue String (companion short story)

THE CLOCKWISE COLLECTION (YA time travel romance)

Casey Donovan has issues: hair, height and uncontrollable trips to the 19th century! And now this ~ she's accidentally taken Nate Mackenzie, the cutest boy in the school, back in time. Awkward.

Clockwise

Clockwiser

Like Clockwork

Counter Clockwise

Clockwork Crazy

Clocked (companion novella)

Standalones

Seaweed

Love, Tink